Geraldine Marie Phipps
1990

Girls to the Front

Also by Vladimir Kornilov

Building a Prison

Vladimir Kornilov

Girls to the Front

Quartet Books

London Melbourne New York

First published in Great Britain by Quartet Books Limited 1985
A member of Namara Group
27/29 Goodge Street, London W1P 1FD

Translated from the Russian, *Devochki i Damochki*
Copyright © 1984 Possev-Verlag

British Library Cataloguing in Publication Data

Kornilov, Vladimir
Girls to the front.
I. Title   II. Devochki i damochki. *English*
891.73′44 F   PG3482.7.R591

ISBN 0-7043-2479-2

Phototypeset by AKM Associates (UK) Ltd.
Ajmal House, Hayes Road, Southall, London
Printed and bound in Great Britain

Principal Characters in
Girls to the Front

Captain Gavrilov: in charge of the trench-digging operation

Sanka ⎫
Liya ⎭ girls in the trench-digging team

Ganya: a middle-aged woman, also in the team

Maria Ivanovna: the girls' 'commander'

Yelena Fedotovna Ryzhova: Ganya's former boss

Karina: Yelena Fedotovna's daughter

Klanka: Ganya's younger sister

Goshka: a teenaged boy

A Red Army truck-driver (formerly a student)

Mikhail Fyodorich: an old man

Serafima (Simka): Gavrilov's wife

Girls to the Front

1

The trench-digging tools arrived just before dawn. Three one-and-a-half-ton trucks crept into the station yard, crunching over the dross, and a gaunt-looking military officer with a captain's badge in his buttonhole stepped out on to the footboard of the first truck and gave a shudder of tiredness.

'Let down the sides!' he shouted, with a wave to the Red Army soldiers who were huddled up in the backs of the trucks.

Some women immediately began to appear from the barracks, shouting to those still inside as they ran: 'Come on girls! There won't be enough spades to go round!'

'Time to wake up!'

Their cries echoed round the yard, and the trucks were immediately surrounded, like mobile shops selling dress-materials.

Well, that's a queer bunch . . . thought the captain, and tried to laugh, but his teeth were chattering too hard. He had been thoroughly chilled during the night, and his body, with its bullet-wounds, did not retain the warmth of a hurriedly snatched gulp of port. He had not lain down all night, and had enough travelling in store that day to last him a good week.

'Girls!' He tried to give a laugh again. 'Come and distribute the tools!'

But his voice was drowned in a sea of laughter and cries of 'Come on,' 'Hey there!' and 'At the double!' Feeling awkward, but at the same time sorry for these women and girls who had woken up earlier than need be, the captain climbed on to the roof of the cabin. From there, having filled his lungs with air, he shouted: 'Quiet, please. Keep calm. Make way for each other!' But the station yard was buzzing as it must have done thirty-odd years earlier during a strike. And the women continued to swarm out of the barracks.

The station was on the outskirts of Moscow, one of a dozen so-called 'dispatch stations' from which citizens, recruited by one means or another for the construction sites in the north and in Siberia, would set off throughout the year. Every autumn short-haired lads would leave here for army service. But since this summer the dispatch station had been working for the front. And now, before daybreak on this chilly October morning, it was crammed full of Muscovites mobilized to dig trenches.

'Oh God. they've brought the spades!' wailed the girls in the barrack where Ganya was sleeping. The doors started banging, and boots, shoes and galoshes began shuffling and stamping over the floorboards. With this ringing in her ears, and a bitter draught blowing from the chinks in the windows, Ganya woke up.

'Damn them, I'd rather sleep,' grumbled some of the girls, turning over and pulling bags or shawls over their heads.

'Just lie where you are!' mumbled a big lass whom Ganya had been lying against during the night. 'It's cold,' she said, and promptly fell asleep. Her thin, red-haired friend, who had kept Ganya warm from the other side, did not wake up at all.

Well, they're conscientious! thought Ganya angrily. From lack of sleep she was furious with the whole world, and especially with this pair, the tubby one and the redhead.

It was only the day before, when Ganya had cursed the woman she kept house for as an 'exploiter' and hurled her ration cards back in her face, that the two girls had 'recruited' her. In tears, Ganya had run out of the courtyard, where several women – including these two girls from the flat opposite – were already standing, with their rucksacks, bags and buckets.

'Don't cry, love,' said Sanka, the fat one, apparently feeling sorry for Ganya.

'Come along with us!' the ginger-haired girl, Liya, had said with a smile. (The witch! thought Ganya now, and intentionally gave her a prod. Liya was sleeping like a drunkard.)

'It'll be good fun!' this 'witch' had said, rather uncertainly, the day before, and the tearful Ganya had yielded and joined up with them. Then a woman by the name of Maria Ivanovna – their 'commander', who was built like a docker – said: 'Attention! Fall in! Quick march!' And as she led them to Nogin Square and then up to the Ilyinksy Gate, she was the first to break into song:

Come on now, my girls!
Come on, my beauties . . .

Ganya set off between the fat girl and the thin girl, and wiping the tears over her wrinkled, unwashed face, joined in the singing:

May the motherland sing about us
And glorify us in song . . .

When they reached the Turkish monument the road flattened out, and marching became easier. They struck up another song, a jollier one, from a film that had been shown free in May at the 'agitation centre':

Nothing will stop us
On sea or on land
We're not afraid
Of ice or clouds . . .

And Ganya recovered completely as she marched along and sang with the rest of them, and even managed to humiliate her former boss in her mind's eye: 'You're doing a bunk, you exploiter, but I'm marching along and singing. I'm a proletarian, but you'll kick the bucket on the road . . . Great bloody beanpole!' (Her boss was very tall.) 'It'll serve you right if you croak . . .'

Ganya smiled with pleasure, and the girls on either side, the redhead and the fat one, urged her on: 'Well done, missus! Great fun, isn't it!'

And thus they had marched through the centre and arrived at the station. Here Ganya's name was registered with the others in a thick school notebook, and then, with all present and correct, they were taken to the mess and given army rations – hot buckwheat porridge with meat, and a mug of tea with two lumps of sugar ('about forty grammes', the women reckoned). The mugs and the bowls were given out through one serving hatch, and the dirty dishes returned to another, and Ganya, perhaps for the first time in her life, did not have to wash up after eating, and lay down proudly in the middle of the barrack between her two new friends. It was warm beside the fat one, and the red-haired one snuggled up trustfully – 'just like a cat' – and Ganya began to fall asleep, feeling happy.

'Pah, go and get lost!' she threatened her mistress. 'You big skinny lamppost. And you're going grey!' She recalled with pleasure that her boss had many grey hairs in her brown plait.

And Ganya had a pleasant dream, set in the Caucasian mountains, where she had been in 1922, at the spa-town of Yessentuki. She dreamed she was riding with her dark-haired sweetheart, Seryoga, in an old-fashioned carriage drawn by a horse with paper ribbons in its mane, as though it had been their wedding. Then they stopped and drank spring water from crystal glasses. Seryoga lazily and tenderly stroked Ganya, and was angry with her younger sister, Klanka, whom Ganya had stupidly brought along with her and who now kept them apart. Ganya felt warm in Seryoga's big hands, but her feet were a little cold and her stomach was queasy, probably from the medicinal water.

And now the early-morning reveille brought Ganya back to the chilly barrack. She stretched her neck painfully, gave a start, and came to on a dirty floor which was crushing her ear.

'Run, missus,' a young lad shouted to her. (This undersized fellow, who was either a volunteer or doing pre-conscription training, had ended up with the women by chance.) 'Run, or you'll end up with a crowbar!'

In fright, Ganya shook herself, grabbed her bag and hurried to the door. Although she was getting on for fifty, she skipped along like a scraggy, awkward little girl who was scared stiff of boys and would play only with other little girls. From the back Ganya still looked young, but her face was wrinkled and her nose had grown long. As if by conspiracy, she had earned the nickname 'Beaky' in every house where she had worked as a charwoman.

'I don't want a crowbar,' she decided as she ran. 'Even a pick would be better.'

It was brighter outside than in the hut. There were electric lights burning, and flames and sparks were flying from shunting engines. The Red Army men on the trucks were slowly handing out the tools. The spades were greased with sticky stuff. 'It's cup grease,' someone explained in the crowd.

Everything will be gone, thought Ganya, and lunged into the crowd with her elbows weaving as though she had missed her stop in a tram. I must get a pick at least – a crowbar will break my hands. But the others knew how to stand up for themselves. After receiving a couple of knocks in the neck and one in the ribs, Ganya gasped: 'Ouch, my bones.' And without even noticing it herself, she left the enemies of fairness and order and joined their defenders.

'Where are you pushing to?' she was soon bawling at one pert girl in a quilted jacket who took it into her head to grasp the side of the truck.

'What's the game, tramping on folk's toes?' she cried at another.

'There's no panic, calm down!' she reasoned with someone else.

'Look at us all,' she sighed, addressing everyone together. 'Hustling and bustling like this! What for? We'll all get something!'

'That's true!' they laughed, 'but how's about you keeping your trap shut, eh?'

A soldier noticed her from the truck and held out a spade. 'Hey, Beaky, catch!'

Ganya jumped up clumsily and snatched at the cold iron spade. No one was bothered. Indeed, the crowd around the lorries had already thinned out, and there turned out to be enough spades for everyone. In fact, there were some left over, and these were dumped with the rest of the gear in a corner of the station yard. The thin captain then climbed into his cabin, and all three trucks turned and drew out through the gates.

The day was slowly breaking. It was that awkward in-between time: too late to sleep, too early for deep conversations about life. Ganya felt depressed again. And her stomach still ached from the previous night's porridge.

I suppose it's my liver again, she sighed to herself as she stood in the empty yard with her foot resting on the shoulder of the spade.

'Digging for spuds?' asked a woman who walked past.

'A grave,' Ganya felt like replying. But the woman had already gone into the barrack. What on earth did I come here for? Free food?! thought Ganya bitterly. Huh! It may be free, but it's bloody awful. They must cook it with machine-oil! She screwed up her face from the pain in her stomach.

And she remembered her twin nephews, her favourites, who had been called up in the summer. They were strapping, handsome lads, like her brother-in-law, Seryoga. What an amount they could put away! They were especially partial to the cold meat from the soup. Ganya used to take them some in an enamelled can from her mistress's, and they would eat it at night after an evening out. Ganya's mistress never touched soup – perhaps she was afraid of

5

catching what d'you call it – gout. And the boss's daughter, Karina, a little girl in specs, also turned up her nose at Ganya's cooking. So Ganya would make good thick soup and hide the meat from it, wrapped in cheesecloth, in her bag. Only later, on the train, would she transfer it to the can. She herself did not eat soup either, preferring Dutch cheese, salami without too much fat, and cocoa (if it was the real stuff, that came in tins, and not that soya substitute, which was too filling).

It was growing light slowly, and the sun was as unwilling to appear as the neighbours in the communal flat were when it came to returning debts to Ganya's boss. They would borrow 150 roubles and bring them back three at a time. The boss was too proud to say anything or let Ganya remind them, and Ganya was heartbroken at the injustice of it. One person would 'forget' to return something, another would pinch paraffin from the kitchen or blacken the primus, or use up the communal firewood to heat water for an extra bath. Ganya remembered all this and took it to heart as if it all belonged to her, not her boss. And in a sense, it *was* hers: what she wasn't given, she took without asking. Sometimes the boss would notice, sometimes not. But even when she did she was embarrassed to say so. Ganya wasn't afraid of her. Whenever she came home, the boss, she would sit down at her typewriter and tap-tap-tap like a machine-gunner. The neighbours said she banged away till two or three in the morning. Ganya herself never spent the night there: she wasn't a servant, after all. She treated it as a place of work, albeit without a contract, but with regular pay and a day off each week. But the neighbours were indignant at the constant clattering, and even complained to the house-manager, and the boss had to upholster her door inside and out with padding and leatherette. The door weighed a ton, and Ganya would kick it open in a temper whenever she was hurrying from the communal kitchen with a boiling kettle or a frying pan.

But no, her job wasn't so bad. Ganya was her own boss. And if Yelena Fedotovna – her mistress – dreamed up some daft scheme like washing sheets ('They haven't been changed for a while.') Ganya felt no need to rush off at once for a basin. Instead, she would stand in the middle of the room (or even better, the kitchen, in front of the neighbours) with her hand under her chin, and carefully consider the matter . . .

'I wonder, you know . . . this probably isn't the right time to do the washing. Maybe nearer the holiday, Yelena Fedotovna, we could . . .' And the boss would hold her tongue and go back to her typewriter to clack away like a salesgirl on a till. It brought in money like a till, too – her main source of income. During the day she was just a schoolteacher.

Yes, it would have been all right if it hadn't been for the war. The war messed everything up.

The first air-raids were barely over before Yelena Fedotovna started pestering her: 'Why don't you go to Kuibyshev* with Karina? I'll send you money.'

'Yelena Fedotovna, I can't just go off and leave my house and plot.'

'House and plot?!' she flared up. Normally she was a quiet person, she kept her voice down and walked about with her head sunk into her shoulders. But now she assumed a jeering tone: 'Half a shed and a bird-table – you call that a house and plot?!'

Ganya cut her off proudly: 'It may be small, but it's mine. All you've got is that rattling old typewriter, and it breaks down twice a week!'

Still, if it hadn't been for the war, life wouldn't have been so bad. But then – her nephews went straight into the army, and her sister, Klanka, was taken to hospital (that's what she gets for playing gooseberry all those years ago!) It looked as if she would not recover: her blood was like water. And hospital food was so awful, you had to take in stuff for her. And on top of that – they brought back rationing again. For everyone except Ganya, that is. She couldn't prove she was a worker (she had no contract) or a dependant. She ran about for a week trying to gather the necessary documents – from Moscow to her home on the Iksha, from the Iksha to Moscow – and in the end just cursed them and gave up. She scraped by as Yelena Fedotovna's housekeeper – there was always some food left after she and Karina had eaten.

And yesterday, suddenly, the boss had dreamed up a new evacuation plan. Now she was going to take Karina herself – without Ganya.

'You'll have to do the washing before we leave!' she commanded.

At that, Ganya shouted at her: 'Washing, indeed! Take that! I'm

---

* City on the Volga to which the Soviet government and many civilians were evacuated during the war. [Tr.]

not your servant!' And she flung her pay back. As for her ration cards, those she screwed up in a ball and threw it at Yelena Fedotovna's face.

Standing now in the station yard, resting on the spade like an old witch with a stick, Ganya gazed at the ground and saw her own life reflected there, bleak and frozen. The only decent thing she could remember was Yessentuki – and look how that ended!

There had never been anything worthwhile in Ganya's life. And now, with her boss gone, it was a dead end.

2

It was still dark when they started serving up pease-porridge and meat. Ganya did not touch them. She just drank tea and sucked some sugar. The ginger-haired girl ate her pease-porridge, but Ganya noticed that she was choking it down with no appetite, just to avoid being conspicuous. The fat girl, on the other hand, polished off her bowl in no time.

'Are there seconds?' she shouted gaily to everyone at her own long table and at the two neighbouring ones.

'Why not? You'll be able to fart louder!'

'It's a man you need, lass, not peas. He could work off some of your fat – before you burst!'

Sanka laughed merrily; she was not offended. It was good to have a laugh at a time like this, before setting out on a cold grey morning, into the unknown. Ganya was also about to make a comment, but Liya, the redhead, spoke first: 'Sanka, take Ganya's. She's not eating.'

'Do you really not want it?' Sanka asked. 'Give us it here then. This cold weather doesn't half make you hungry.'

'Hey,' Ganya snapped, 'keep your paws to yourself. It's not yours. And you,' she flew at Liya, 'you keep your beady eyes off other people's things. I know your type.'

'You bitch,' said Sanka, spitefully banging her spoon against her mug as she stirred her tea.

Liya blushed, but said nothing. She had vowed to be the same as everyone else, not to stand out, and to swallow any offence. For three years now she had tried to be like the crowd, or, if possible, a little better. She did everything she could to stop blushing, but lacked the power. Her face turned crimson.

Liya, a Komsomol member, had resigned herself to everything. At first her family had a two-roomed flat. Her mother was fit, they had a housekeeper, and her father had access to a special closed shop. Her father would come home in the evenings by car, in a good mood, wearing his narrow blue breeches tucked into soft kid boots and a blue field-shirt with a broad belt. He would kiss Liya and nod to her mother. He was a rather portly, imposing figure, and his semi-military uniform became him – a factory director – well.

And suddenly, one misfortune followed another: her mother fell ill, her father was sacked, and one of their rooms was taken from them (it was given to the fat girl, Sanka, her drunken father, who was the house-manager, and her noisy, quarrelsome mother, who kept the yard). They had to give up their housekeeper, as they had little enough room for themselves. They had already sold off what they could through the State commission shops, and the rest Liya and Sanka (who proved to be a very sympathetic person) carted off to sell at the 'flea-market' at weekends. Her mother, since she had fallen in the toilet, was confined to her bed and had to be nursed like a baby. And more and more often her father started jeering and mocking at her mother. He simply could not cope with invalids – his nerves gave out. Nor was he used to being idle. He was a born industrialist, a 'Red director. And now, locked up at home, he was transformed into a pitiful, cantankerous, nasty man. He was terribly resentful at the neighbours for taking away his study, but was the first to greet Sanka's drunk father when they met, and would even offer him a cigarette. But then he complained that the house-manager was forever cadging a smoke from him. 'I can't afford to keep him in cigarettes,' he would say, and insist on smoking in their own room. His wife, though ill, would not allow him to open a window, as she had a temperature.

She had always had trouble with her vegetative nervous system. She had grown up in a cultured family and, according to her relations, was very musical. Even before the present crisis, her nerves had sometimes played up and she had even had fits, but at that time it had been up to the housekeepers to deal with them, whereas now it was up to Liya's father. Yet here he was, smoking in front of her. Liya could do nothing with him. Cigarettes were very expensive, and her mother extremely unwell, but her father was so touchy that he flew into a rage at the gentlest of hints.

He did not lose weight immediately, but grew sort of greyish and flabby. He now felt ashamed to wear his semi-military uniform, and his civilian three-piece suit, which dated back to the NEP period,* was so tight and old-fashioned that he looked positively suspicious in it. Liya's father really did expect serious trouble during the eighteen months his wife lay dying. Word reached Liya's school that he had lost his job, and some of the pupil's suggested 'investigating' Liya at a Komsomol meeting. But before the term was up she left school and found work at a library, where there were only neat old ladies working and there was no need to register with the Komsomol.

Throughout the eighteen months, her father was quite unbearable. But Liya loved him. She was proud of him and sorry for him. She knew he was not guilty of anything, and that he was a talented – a natural! – manager. He was born to it. He simply had some enemy, who envied him because he was talented. And Soviet power would protect him. Liya's father appealed to the Moscow Party organization, and to the Central Committee, and to the Party Control Committee. Then he wrote personally to Comrade Stalin.

Liya herself asked him to write. She corrected his mistakes and personally delivered the letter. It was only her confidence that kept him going. His daughter was cast in his own mould, and during that year and a half she was even stronger than he.

'Just you wait,' she would say to him, sitting on the edge of his bed before going to sleep. 'You know there are a lot of saboteurs about – it's very hard to trust people just now. But they *will* look into your case. We'll just have to wait a little.'

Then she would get up from his bed, make her own bed on the floor, and go over to her mother in another corner of the room. She would change her mother's nightclothes and give her something

* The New Economic Policy (NEP) reintroduced elements of capitalism into the Soviet economy during the twenties. The implication is that Liya's father was one of the small businessmen who flourished at the time, and that his suit looked conspicuously 'bourgeois'. [Tr.]

to drink, and then take her temperature, but always show her a different thermometer which never rose above 37.2

'Everything will be fine with Dad,' Liya would reassure her.

That was how it was for a whole year and a half, while her mother was dying. But then justice was done: her father was rehabilitated and appointed chief engineer of a construction trust in the Urals. He put on his breeches and field-shirt again (though they were too big for him now) and without waiting for his wife's death set off for Chelyabinsk. Liya's mother was determined not to go to hospital, and since Liya worked shifts, Sanka often looked after her.

In short, Liya learned to put up with everything: with leaving school early, with her mother's whining, with the despondency at home and her father's nervousness, and finally with her father's departure and her mother's death.

But she never learned to stop herself blushing.

'Forget it,' said Sanka, giving her a hug. 'And you can choke!' she bellowed across the table at Ganya. 'I don't want your breakfast. I'm full.'

And then Ganya started snivelling and twitching her long nose.

'Can't fathom you at all,' said the woman next to her.

'A professor couldn't fathom the likes of her,' sighed another.

'Yes, a woman is like a chemist's shop – you can't understand a thing without a good drink!' added another, and the conversation almost got sidetracked as Ganya continued to sniff and tears ran down her lined face.

'Listen,' Ganya finally managed to splutter out a few words. 'I don't grudge you it. Eat it, Sanka. I'm not allowed that kind of thing – because of my liver,' she explained, as though confiding in everyone and raising them to her level. 'When I was young I used to eat like a horse, but now – I've got this liver complaint . . . It could be cancer, or angina, or goodness knows what – the doctors are blind . . . What I could do with is some cheese . . . Anyway, you eat it!' She spun the bowl across the table to Sanka. 'And Liya, you should eat up too, even if you have to force it down – tomorrow it'll be even worse.'

Some of the other women tut-tutted: 'Give us a break, Beaky!'

'Stop crowing, for God's sake!'

'Finish eating!' shouted Maria Ivanovna, the huge woman in

charge of their detachment – the 'commander'. 'Our train will be here in a minute.'

Again the women started bustling about as they had when the trench-digging gear had arrived. Ganya dashed into the barrack, grabbed her bag and spade, and for want of anything else to do, sank down on the floor.

The other women also ran to seize their bags, sacks, spades and pails, and then hung around indecisively.

'This is no time for sunbathing! Out into the yard and fall in!' commanded the military officer who had arrived with the trucks during the night, and had now appeared at the door.

It was quite light outside now, but the sky was heavily overcast.

'At least there shouldn't be any planes about,' said some of the women, yawning.

'Line up!' shouted the captain. He again climbed awkwardly on to the cabin of his truck. This time there was only one truck. What's he here for? Ganya wondered.

'He's brought gloves!' said the undersized volunteer from nearby, as though he had read her thoughts.

'That's to save our silky-soft hands!' There was laughter all round.

'Come on, you chatterboxes! Fall in!' commanded the captain. They lined up clumsily.

'Will detachment commanders put some order into these ranks!' shouted the thin officer. 'Come on, straighten up there! Atten-shun! Ah, why do I bother? Stand as you are!' He gave a dismissive wave of his sleeve. 'Quiet! Listen to me,' he raised his voice. 'Comrade women! The situation is very serious. The enemy are penetrating to the very heart of our country.'

He wanted to say something particularly heartfelt and kind to them, because he felt sorry for them, exhausted as they were by this sleepless night in a cold station barrack – quite apart from their everyday cares. He felt like, if not exactly cheering them up, at least saying something jocular. But as soon as he got up on the cabin roof he remembered a verse from a Nazi leaflet which had been read out at the previous day's briefing session:

> Russian ladies, don't waste your time
> Digging trenches for your men.
> Soon our tanks will come along
> And fill your trenches in again.

Yesterday, the verse had not struck him as anything particularly worth worrying about. And the dozen or so other commanders sitting in the civilian Tozhanov's cramped room had also exchanged surprised glances.

But today, faced with his own 'Russian ladies', who were being sent out from Moscow, nearer to those tanks which he knew only too well, the captain felt ill at ease, and stopped short . . .

'Anyway, er, share out the picks and crowbars. Leaders, pick groups of ten. Each ten is a squad. Everything clear?'

'Everything clear,' echoed a confusion of voices.

'Keep in formation! I'll soon be back to inspect you,' added the captain, half-menacingly, half-sadly, before climbing down. 'OK,' he said to the driver, as he got in beside him, and the truck crawled out through the gates.

'Stay where you are,' shouted the group-leaders. 'Number off in tens!'

'Quickly!' Maria Ivanovna snapped at her group. 'The Germans are coming!'

'They won't. It's too cloudy!' said the little fellow in Ganya's row with a laugh. Seeing him now in the daylight, Ganya was amazed she had not recognized him earlier. It was Goshka, from Karina's class – a friend of the little 'wonder-child'.

'Number off!' ordered Maria Ivanovna.

Liya and Sanka were numbers eight and nine, and Ganya number ten, the last in the squad. One more, and she would have been with strangers. There must be a God! she thought with relief.

'Right, you take up the most space around here,' Maria Ivanovna said to Sanka. 'You see to this lot – and keep them like *this*!' She curled her stubby fingers into a fair-sized fist. 'Take ten pairs of mittens, and make sure they take the picks and crows. Otherwise all these weaklings will try and get away with just spades. Right?'

'Ay-ay, sir!' Sanka replied gaily, and smartly raised her hand to her kerchief.

3

There were open trucks and heated goods-vans on the train when it arrived, but the girls were lucky enough to find an ordinary passenger compartment, with two berths and a third for luggage. Ganya had guessed where to stand, and when the carriage stopped in front of her she grasped the hand-rail, jumped inside, and reserved two window-seats; one for herself and the one opposite for Maria Ivanovna.

'Huh!' Maria Ivanovna gestured to Ganya. 'I've got no time to sit about!'

It was as if she had had a premonition. Immediately a howl went up over the city – and probably over the whole region.

'Citizens, this is an air-raid warning!' said one of the girls in the next compartment, imitating the deep voice of a well-known radio announcer.

So much for the clouds! thought Ganya. She looked out of the window, but could see nothing because they were hard up against a warehouse.

Since July the women had more or less grown accustomed to the air-raids. Although Moscow had been bombed it was a very big city – and besides, you can't see bombs falling when you are in the underground or a shelter. And not everyone has the time or inclination to travel about to see what has been destroyed. On the other hand a downed German bomber had been put on display in the city centre, on Revolution Square, and everybody had seen that. So by October people were no longer so terrified by air-raids.

But now, torn away from their families, enclosed in these railway compartments with their bundles and suitcases, the women felt uncomfortable and uneasy. It was not just a physical crampedness: they felt it inside too. Above them the whining went on and on, and although they could hear no explosions as yet – or even any anti-aircraft fire – each one imagined a direct hit – right on this carriage, this compartment, on me . . .

The howl of the sirens seemed to sound directly above the women's heads, and those on the top bunks wished they could get lower down. But those on the bottom berths imagined the track being blown up below them, and they felt like jumping out on to the station platform.

'Don't panic!' cried Maria Ivanovna from the door, although nobody was panicking. The women huddled closely together.

'Move off quickly,' she shouted down the platform, apparently to one of the engine-drivers.

'Stay in your seats! Don't panic!' she called into the tense carriage, and folded double the broad army belt she wore around her long green quilted jacket, just in case she had to quell any disturbance.

' "She's got a revolver under her skirt"!' sang the young lad, Goshka. He was sitting next to Ganya, puffing at a stump of a cigarette.

I wish I did have a revolver, thought Maria Ivanovna. In a responsible position like mine a revolver would give me greater authority . . .

'Give's a light!' she cried to Goshka. 'And put yours out. You're too young!'

'Quite right,' Ganya agreed, making up to the chief. 'Put it out – it's stuffy in here. And you shouldn't be smoking anyway. Once you're a soldier you can smoke away till you're killed.'

'Leave the lad alone,' said Sanka. 'Come and sit here.' She moved away from the window and let Goshka in. 'Only open the window a bit first. There now, that's better.'

The sound of singing, rather out of tune, floated in from an open truck coupled to the carriage:

> Do you love me, little bird,
> Will you help me, dove?

And a weak voice in the next compartment took up the song, but petered out again when no one joined in:

> Fly away and find my man,
> Send him all my love . . .

'There's a draught,' Ganya complained. 'And don't you bother giving him your seat. I only gave you it temporarily – until the chief wants it.' She turned respectful.y to Maria Ivanovna who was standing in the doorway holding her belt, like a cossack with a whip.

'Shut up, missus, or I really will thump you one,' said Sanka with a yawn. 'Time we were moving, isn't it? Do you want a smoke, love?' She gave Liya an affectionate hug. Liya shook her head and pressed against her. Suddenly the train moved off.

'Oh God, I wish it was over,' someone sighed, and some girls on the upper bunks crossed themselves.

'Phew!' said Maria Ivanovna, and sat down on the edge of the seat, having fastened her belt again.

The train was gathering speed. The sirens still droned on, and anti-aircraft guns could now be heard, as well as what sounded like bombs exploding somewhere. But over the regular rumbling of the wheels it did not sound quite so bad.

'I've kept you a window-seat,' Ganya smiled to her chief again. 'Get up and give her a seat,' she said to Goshka.

'Leave him. The seats aren't reserved,' replied Maria Ivanovna. 'Maybe he'll have to do some soldiering soon. Do you know how to shoot?'

Goshka nodded without taking out his cigarette.

'You'll come in handy. Remind me. They should be issuing us with weapons,' Maria Ivanovna lied, with an important air. Although she was entrusted with some kind of authority and was on familiar terms with all the district commanders, nobody had promised her any arms, and she could not even handle a gun.

'Give me and Liya them, too,' said Sanka. 'We've done basic training.'

'All right, we'll see. What about you, Beaky?'

'What would I want a gun for? Give me a frying pan – I can cook.'

'My, that's a rare talent!' laughed the woman sitting next to her. The train had now left the outskirts of Moscow, and the atmosphere on board grew more cheerful.

Some of the girls in the open truck started singing:

The city we love may soundly sleep . . .

'Do you work in a canteen? The chief looked at Ganya. 'I don't seem to recognize your face. I meant to ask you when I was taking your name. Are you from their block?'

'Uh-huh,' Ganya nodded, not mentioning the canteen. 'From number twenty-seven.'

'Ah. That's opposite your flat,' said Maria Ivanovna, nodding to Liya and Sanka. 'So you mean you're a servant? Not registered there?'

'She doesn't live in,' said Liya quietly.

'And where are you from yourself?'

'From out of town. Mrs Ryzhova – Yelena Fedotovna – asked me to come and look after her daughter Karina. We're old friends . . . Karina's eyesight . . .'

'Do you mean that tall woman? The one who types all the time? Strange family, that.'

'What's strange about it?' Goshla leapt to her defence. 'She's a teacher and a qualified typist.'

'Nobody asked you. So you're friends, you say?' asked Maria Ivanovna, puffing smoke at Ganya. 'Been friends for long?'

'Oh, yes, a long time. I've got my own place. But I feel sorry for Karina. She has to eat regular meals – her eyesight is useless.'

'And where's Ryzhova's husband?' The 'commander' narrowed her eyes and then opened her mouth with pleasure, as though she had taken aim and got a bull's eye.

'She doesn't have a husband,' said Ganya in surprise. 'What does she need one for? She's a serious woman. Doesn't bother with men.'

'I suppose the wind blew in her daughter!' There was laughter on the upper berths.

'Who asked you?' Ganya craned her neck to see them. 'Give people peace to talk. She doesn't have a husband,' she turned back to Maria Ivanovna. 'There was one Armenian . . . we went to Armenia together once. Well, that's where it happened . . .' Ganya was making up this story, without knowing why. 'I told her: "Get rid of it!" but she was scared, just like my sister Klanka. So she just had the baby.'

'Ah,' said the commander. 'I'd heard a different story. You've got a good block of flats, a clean block. We wouldn't want the wrong sort of people living there. When your Ryzhova moved in I was pleased because it meant those – what d'you call them – moving out – that granny with the young kids. But then I was told that Ryzhova was also, er . . . So they were lying, were they?'

'Uh-huh,' Ganya trembled, much to Goshka's delight. 'No, she's a serious woman, a typist.'

What am I protecting her for? Ganya thought to herself.

Ryzhova, too, eh? I'd never have gone and worked for her if I'd known . . . Never mind, they'll uncover her murky deeds yet!

Liya sat pressed up against the side of the compartment, and had a sinking feeling inside. Poor Yelena Fedotovna, she thought. Such a warm-hearted and intelligent woman. And Karina, even though she's just a little girl, and very selfish, is also a very interesting person already.

She's a fool, thought the young volunteer, Goshka, sitting opposite Ganya. She's a fool, but she's wriggled out of it. There's something doglike about servants, or rather, slavelike. Like Oblomov's servant, Zakhar. They slang their masters, but won't let anyone else do it. And look at this one. (He glanced at Maria Ivanovna.) She's got her head screwed on – a real Stateswoman!

And Goshka remembered with distaste how the day before she had refused to let him walk separately from the women. He had had to march right in the middle of the column of singing women, choking with shame. Hm! You ask to go to the front, and people like her send you to dig trenches! Well, never mind, it'll be easier to escape to the front from there! At that thought, he cheered up and tentatively squeezed up to Sanka.

'So you're a housekeeper, then?' yawned the chief. 'Without a contract, I suppose?'

'I didn't have time to have one drawn up,' Ganya nodded, feeling humiliated.

'She's a spy,' taunted Goshka, now in a jolly mood. 'You'd better keep your eye on her!'

Again there was laughter up above.

'I'll give you a bloody spy,' retorted Ganya.

'Right, you lot, carry on laughing without me. I'm off to see how the others are getting on.' Maria Ivanovna set off down the corridor, and the first compartment became a little less cramped.

'Move up, Sanka,' grinned Ganya. 'The poor lad's like a beetroot. You're squashing him!'

'So what? Let him warm up a bit! Give me your hand, Goshka!' The fat girl laughed and took hold of Goshka's hand, as though she intended to place it inside her padded jacket.

The upper berths guffawed, and Liya gave a false titter.

'Leave me!' said an embarrassed Goshka, withdrawing his hand.

'Don't be shy – I mean well,' beamed Sanka. 'If you feel cold, go ahead – it's perfectly natural!'

'Give over,' the volunteer growled, not sure whether to take offence or to laugh along with the others. He liked the plump girl.

'He's already earmarked for Karina,' said Ganya. 'You're too big for him.'

The train was now well outside of Moscow. The sirens could no longer be heard – only the bursts of anti-aircraft fire.

Goshka stuck his head out of the window. 'They're giving them hell!' he said.

'Pooh! You'll soon have seen enough of that!' said Sanka with a shudder.

'They should be fighting them with planes,' sighed the woman at the end of Ganya's seat. 'What's the point of shooting at them from the ground? It's like giving drops to a dead man.'

'Drops!' exclaimed Goshka angrily. 'A single splinter's enough to bring a plane down. Especially if you hit the fuel tank.'

'And how do you propose to do that?' responded a deeper voice from above. 'It's not going to stand still for you!'

'They send up a barrage of defensive fire,' explained Liya in a strained voice.

'Ah? Oh, I see what you mean,' replied the voice. 'My nephew's an anti-aircraft gunner. He came to see us last week. He says one shell costs as much as a pair of calf-leather boots. D'you hear that? Think how many pairs have gone up in smoke!'

'We can spare it – we're rich!' said Sanka, and pushed her feet, in their patched-up men's shoes, under the seat. Everyone laughed.

Then a serious voice drifted in from the next compartment: 'This is a war. Once we've won we can count the cost.'

'People are most important of all,' Liya declared, at last overcoming her shyness. 'The anti-aircraft batteries are there to defend Moscow – all of us . . .' She wanted to add, 'and Comrade Stalin', but felt embarrassed.

'Once we win we can count the cost,' someone repeated in the next compartment.

'But they could at least have given us one pair of boots,' Ganya thought aloud. 'I've got two nephews – they didn't even give them boots, just shoes and thick bandages . . .'

'Oh, I'm sure they're worth a pair of sandals as well,' said Goshka.

'Ooh, you creep,' Ganya sounded hurt. 'Hit him, Sanka! Sandals! My nephews aren't like you – they're real soldiers. Seduced every girl on the Iksha, they did.'

'He-men!' whistled the volunteer.

'The Germans are strong,' said one of the girls above Ganya. 'We need more than boots to beat them. They fight with their heads.'

'What are you prattling about?' retorted someone on the berth opposite.

'You call it prattling, but I know . . . So keep your mouth shut. See for yourself where we're going.'

'Where? Where? It's a military secret where we're going.'

'Secret? Do you think we're going to Berlin? Eighty miles – that's our limit.'

'Don't bother counting the miles,' said an invisible woman in the next compartment. 'Napoleon got further than the Germans – and what happened?'

'Napoleon's not a good example,' said Goshka, taking out his cigarette.

'What's Napoleon got to do with it?' Sanka let fly. 'Look at the troops we've got in Moscow. The whole road to Gorky is packed with Red Army soldiers and tanks. The road to Yaroslavl's the same. And the Kazan road looks like an armoured train.'

'Exactly,' Goshka agreed, although he had not set foot outside of Moscow all summer or autumn.

It's probably true, thought Liya. Sanka must have been told so by someone.

'They're powerful, though,' said the serious woman from next door. 'The Germans are gathering everything for the last decisive battle, and then they'll roll forward.'

'That's right. And you're counting how many miles away they are,' said Sanka, raising her head.

'That's not what I'm saying,' the girl answered above. 'What I'm saying is that the Germans are stupid. It's as easy to fool them as spitting.'

'Go and spit then, for God's sake!' said Sanka, again causing laughter all around.

'But you're missing the point,' the same voice went on. 'They're stupid. It's easy to dupe them. We had refugees living with us for two days – they told us how stupid the Germans are. You can run rings round them. And even nick things from them – no bother at all.'

'So what did your refugees run away for?' asked Ganya in surprise.

'What do you mean "what for"? Because they're Soviet citizens. Who wants to live under an enemy? But that's beside the point. What I'm saying is the Germans are stupid. You can outwit them. These refugees of ours – their son nicked a helmet, and a gun – one of them little rifle things – and two bars of chocolate! And he got away with it. They believed it wasn't him! And the daughter, she was a good-looking girl, like you,' she pointed down at Sanka. 'An officer wanted to rape her – she told him she had a bad disease, and he left her alone. He believed her!'

'The Germans are fascists. They're occupying our country, and they're no better than animals,' said a voice in the other compartment.

'That's exactly what I'm saying,' continued the woman on the top bunk. 'You can fool a German. He only looks straight ahead, never sideways. He's only got ears at the sides of his head – and they don't understand Russian.'

'They shouldn't have bothered running away, then,' said Ganya.

'You're a defeatist,' Goshka lost his temper. 'We'll never win with the likes of you.'

'Shut your trap!' Ganya countered.

'Just look at you! First you stole from the Ryzhovs, now you hope to do the same with the Germans.'

'Ooh, you little bugger, I'll . . .' Ganya flew at him.

'Keep calm, dear,' Sanka intervened. 'The Germans won't want you. They like their women clean. And I bet you haven't paid a visit to the bathhouse since last year!'

'I haven't noticed you there, either. You didn't scrub my back.'

'That's right,' Sanka agreed. 'I wash kids at the kindergarten. The likes of you get washed in a morgue.'

'So there!' The volunteer burst out laughing.

They should be ashamed of themselves, thought Liya. But they all mean well. There's something genuine in all of them, even in poor old Ganya. Look at how she marched and sang yesterday. There is courage and selflessness in even the very worst people. It just has to be uncovered – uncovered in everyone at the same time: then we would be victorious. And we shouldn't be arguing. We need good leaders. Maria Ivanovna is good, but she can't carry people along with her. She relies on giving orders. You need a warmer person – someone like Sanka. Sanka's a real leader. If only

I could converse with people like that. But I can't. I'm plain, and gauche. Nobody would listen to me.

'Don't be sad, sweetheart,' someone said to Ganya from above. 'All you need is a good wash, a bow in your hair, and a tray – you'll be all right!'

'What are you attacking me for? What have I done?' Ganya started crying. 'I've got nephews at the front!'

'What's all the noise about? Not fighting, are you?' asked Maria Ivanovna gaily, returning from her inspection. 'Shove up a bit!' She pushed Liya. 'I'd better sit down for a minute – there might not be another chance for a while.'

4

They were detrained in the middle of a field, about three kilometres before a bombed station.

'Come on!'

'Quickly!' The train's crew were growing nervous on the exposed embankment.

'But it's awkward!' the women tried to justify themselves.

'Awkward! Look at that station over there! Blown to smithereens!'

The woman's buckets clanged and their spades rang as they fell on the ground.

'Ow, I've twisted my foot!'

'Ouch, my heel!'

'I'll hurt myself!'

It was particularly difficult to clamber out of the goods-van.

'Easy does it!' said the train-driver and stoker as they helped the girls out. 'Now run like hell over that field, before they come back again!' They looked up uneasily at the greyish sky.

There was only a slight wind, but it was a desolate kind of day. The trench-diggers set off straight across an unpicked potato field.

'Keep in your tens!' commanded the squad-leaders, but the women found it impossible to march in formation through the potato-tops. Their feet kept sinking into the soft, thawing earth and slipping on the potatoes.

'They're just going to waste!' sighed some of the women regretfully.

'Fill your hems with them! We'll bake them later.'

'They've probably been spoiled by the frost.'

Be that as it may, many of the women tried to pick up some of the unearthed potatoes as they stumbled along.

'Left! Left!' roared the squad-leaders. 'No time for that!'

'Jump to it! Jump to it!' mimicked Ganya angrily, not because she was especially keen on potatoes, but simply because it was hard walking over the uneven field with a pick and a spade. And because she had been picked on in the train.

They're all so bloody clever, she complained, but when they start digging their cleverness won't be much good to them . . . Oh well – left, right, left, right . . . She trampled on the frozen potato-tops.

The sun was stuck behind the clouds, as though it were also afraid of the German planes. Beyond the field stood a white church, with an asphalted road winding past it.

It would be good to have an artillery observation post on the church, thought good Goshka, who was walking apart from the women. You could have a telephone link with it, or even wireless . . . an aerial instead of a cross! Tremendous! 'Gun number one – fire! Gun number two – fire!' he commanded to himself as he plodded through the sticky earth. When the Red Army takes over the trenches I'll stay behind with them . . . He could already visualize the completed trenches, the barbed wire, and the anti-tank barriers on the road that snaked past the village church. There's probably a river behind it, he thought. I read somewhere that they always built churches above rivers. Those religious fools certainly knew how to choose a good spot for defending themselves. I'll stay behind here. Karina's been evacuated anyway . . . And he recalled how he and Karina had climbed on to their roof to put out any incendiary bombs that might fall. But they were out of luck – nothing fell on their block. None the less Karina's mother turned on a show of hysterics for him. Her face was all white, and she took valerian, and once she had calmed down, apologized: 'You must understand, Goshka. You see, Karina's all I've got – there's nobody else, you know.' And he promised not to take Karina on to the roof again. The following evening he even went to the air-raid shelter with her . . . Yelena Fedotovna's not so bad, he thought.

But Karina, quite honestly, is wonderful. Her short-sightedness will pass. She should wear glasses, just to strengthen her eyesight. And she shouldn't read lying down, the silly thing . . .

Liya could barely drag herself along in her yellow knee-length laced boots, carrying a bucket and her bag on the spade across her shoulder. Her heels kept sticking in the muddy soil and she was tired of having to pull them out. She was irritated by these old boots of her mother's, and wished she had sold them years ago at the market. But her mother had been determined not to let them go cheaply. She always hoped they would come back into fashion, and she could have worn them again herself – if her feet stopped being so swollen. Her mother was incredibly stubborn. And now Liya was angry with Sanka – for advising her to put on the monstrous things. 'I'd love to wear them myself,' Sanka had assured Liya the day before, 'if only I could get into them!'

As she trudged across the sticky field, Liya pictured Moscow's Central Park on the last Sunday evening before the war. Sanka had virtually had to drag her there. She was sleeping in Liya's room by then (six months after her mother's death): she had transferred her own bedclothes to Liya's mother's bed, and even hung a pinafore and a couple of dresses in Liya's wardrobe.

'Come on, let's go!' Sanka had insisted. Liya did not even change – she had nothing to change into. (Liya grudged spending the money her father sent on clothes. She paid it into a savings bank, thinking it would come in handy if she managed to take her school exams externally and go on to college. Now it would lie in the bank until the war was over.) To cut a long story short, she went to the park only to accompany Sanka, since it was better for a girl not to walk alone in a park. Sanka, though a year younger, was already hankering after boys. And now an opportunity presented itself – the room was free. It was because of the room that she asked me to go with her, thought Liya as she watched Sanka gaily striding over the potato field ahead of her. Well, what would you expect? She's a nice-looking girl – good fun!

'Don't touch us; we shan't touch you!' Liya could not help smiling as she remembered how Sanka had chanted this to ward off some 'worthless' admirers that evening in the park. Some of the boys were actually not bad at all, but Sanka just brushed them aside. The things she said were pure drivel, but turned out amusing and apt. Her six years at school never let her down in conversation, whereas Liya with her nine years (less a term) could barely utter a word.

After a shower of rain it was even rather pleasant to walk along the reddish paths, but Sanka was forever dragging Liya away – first to the bandstand, surrounded by people singing together like children, then to the little dance floor where they were doing the foxtrot – in a word, to the people and the bright lights, where Liya's worn-out tennis shoes and skinny white freckly arms were all the more visible.

The boys were also walking about in twos or threes. It was easier for them to pick up girls that way because they could show off in front of each other. But as soon as they way Liya – it seemed to her – they all cooled down, and after a couple of words they would raise their palms and wave them in the air: '*Auf Wiedersehen!*'

'I'm going,' Liya would bleat. 'I'm just spoiling everything for you!'

'No, never mind. There'll be others!' Sanka would give her a hug, and seemed genuinely confident. And to be sure, she got what she wanted.

'Over there, look!' She prodded Liya in the side. 'Will they do? Which do you want – Kryuchkov or Abrikosov?'

Two chaps were strolling lazily beside a pond – one stocky with a light-brown forelock, the other dark and tall. That was about the extent of their similarity to the aforementioned film stars.

'You're joking!' Liya shrank back. 'They're not your types!' she almost said, but refrained from it. No, these lads, of course, were not suitable for Sanka. They had extraordinarily pleasant, cultured faces – that struck one immediately. The fair-haired one looked like a sports champion on a poster, and the other was obviously a student. There was a sort of pensive sadness in his eyes, as though he knew more than others about life and even somehow kept aloof from it all. And they were dressed almost too well, both in neatly pressed trousers and silk shirts, and both in proper shoes, not sandals: the fair-haired one's were made of white canvas, the tall one's of dark-brown leather.

'Don't, Sanka.' Liya took her by the arm.

'Don't be so timid,' she retorted. 'The main thing is, don't let them see you're shy. Are we Muscovites or are we not?'

The boys happened to stop beside a mobile stall selling aerated water.

'Well, students, a drop of H_2O, eh? Is it any good?' Sanka spoke patronizingly and casually, as though she were addressing her kindergarten tiny tots, not young men. Liya felt her cheeks must have turned redder than the pathway. Just as well it was not a very bright day.

'She's shy!' Sanka grinned, giving Liya a slap on the shoulder. 'She's thirsty, but she's watching her figure. One glass a day is her limit. We were just wondering what the water here was like.'

'Buy them a drink, Viktor, and let's go,' growled the athlete. 'This isn't Rio de Janeiro.' He went away from the stall.

'What's that? You wouldn't recommend a *crème brûlée*?' Sanka chattered on.

'You idiot! That was meant as an insult!' Liya felt like crying.

'They're in a hurry,' Sanka laughed. 'These students don't worry about food.'

'You fool – they don't want to know you,' Liya forced the words out.

'Oh, stop hissing like a snake.'

'I'm sorry, he's out of sorts,' said the dark-haired youth. 'Zhorka, come here!' The athlete did not turn round.

If it hadn't been for me, Viktor would have gone too, thought Liya as she stumbled over the sticky field, brushing past the potato-tops in her laced boots.

The women were stretched out in a line from the embankment to the main road. Their bags swung about on their spades, and their buckets clanged.

'Head straight for the church, you atheists!' shouted Maria Ivanovna, the squad-leader.

I suppose I was closer to him spiritually, but Sanka was more of a woman, thought Liya. She could not help admiring Sanka as she boldly trampled over the potatoes in her father's shoes. Even in her short skirt, worn over ski-pants, and her padded jacket she looked fine. You'd think she was strolling through a park. You don't even notice her spade and crowbar . . . Hm, funny things, people!

'Here you are. It's our telephone number. We live alone,' Sanka had said to Viktor after he had accompanied them to the Park of Culture metro station. For a whole two hours the three of them had wandered round the park. Sanka had immediately taken the student's arm, and Liya had had to walk at Sanka's side, which made it very inconvenient for her to talk to the young man. In any case, Sanka would not let her get a word in edgeways.

'Quit this serious stuff! Literature, literature! Dries you up, that stuff – or ruins your eyesight, like our neighbour Karina.' She yawned intentionally. Liya felt she was intruding, and blushed, and kept trying to leave them alone, but Sanka hung on to her arm too, and would not let her go. She literally clung to them, always cheerful and lusty, and at the same time sly and smart – never offensive without call, but always insisting on getting her own way. Meanwhile the student (whom, Liya divined, was not only sad, but also shy) could think of no way to unhook himself.

'So do give us a ring,' said Sanka at the metro in a voice full of unambiguous promise, and all but kissed the young man.

'You really are a good pal,' she said, embracing Liya as they stood on the escalator. 'Without you he'd have got away! It's a good thing you work in a library. You should bring me something sometime to have a look at . . .'

By now the most agile women had reached the church. They were almost all carrying buckets, and Ganya breathlessly tried to keep up with them, assuming that they were going to be the cooks.

'Over here,' shouted the thin captain, pointing to the open doors of the church. Behind him was his dark-coloured one-and-a-half-ton truck.

Bloody magician! thought Ganya. He's like a sailor – one day here, another day there! And who's the old codger he's picked up?

A little old man in glasses and a long trenchcoat, like those worn by escorts or government officials, was hovering round the officer, waving his arms about and arguing about something.

'I can envisage an observation post on the church, Comrade Captain,' the old man was enthusing. 'The outlook is exceptional!'

The captain did not reply. His thoughts were elsewhere.

'We'll dig up the whole riverbank. The bridges, both the railway and the road bridges, I think, will have to be blown up. And we'll put anti-tank barriers on the main road – we can cut up the rails and weld them together for that.'

'So long as it's not a botched-up do-it-yourself job. I've seen enough amateur stuff today,' the captain said with his teeth clenched.

'No, no. We'll use the narrow-gauge track for it – it's just rusting away over there to no purpose'.

'Hm, why not? Go ahead,' agreed the captain. 'But make sure they don't botch it . . . Were you, er, in the civil-defence corps?' he asked out of politeness, tearing himself away from his unhappy thoughts for a moment.

'I studied it,' said the old man hesitantly. But the captain had no time to find out more.

'Bring the gear over here!' he shouted to the approaching women and signalled to the church with a wave of his hand. 'I've brought provisions. Go and collect them from the truck – but calmly! On second thoughts, leave them – let the squad-leaders sort them out.'

If there was another train there, he thought, I'd send them all back to the capital. There's nothing for them to do here. Superstitiously, he felt sorry for the women, in the hope that there would be good men over there, beyond the front, too, who would take pity on his wife and children.

In the meantime the old man had popped into the church, which was evidently being used as a repair-shop, because just then some boys came out with two wheelbarrows, each bearing a cylinder. Whooping with delight, they wheeled them across to the sparse woods beyond the main road.

Well, thought the captain, it's better they're busy than idle. Idleness generates panic and disorder. You're less afraid when you're busy . . . Who knows, perhaps we'll manage to halt them here . . .

But a desperate sadness was gnawing at his heart.

5

The day had got off to a bad start at the dispatch station, when they had refused to issue him with provisions. All they would give was one load of bread per person and some compound lard, but not enough for all three hundred women.

'Bureaucrats!' The captain tried to put pressure on them. 'What am I supposed to do – send an empty truck a hundred kilometres?'

'No, captain,' interrupted the quartermaster, an elderly, dumpy little man, re-enlisted after the war broke out. Four triangles protruded from behind the starched collar of his overalls. 'We've got more than just your women to feed. This is a mess, not a warehouse. We feed you here, but you'll have to get provisions from the base.'

'They used to issue them here.'

'That's as may be; but not any more.'

'Look, sergeant-major, there's still a war on.' The captain raised his voice, half-ordering him, and half-trying to win him round. 'I'm telling you: give us our meal and our lard.'

'No,' repeated the sergeant-major.

'I am ordering you! Full stop!'

'No.' The sergeant-major shook his spiky grey head.

'Refusing to obey orders! I'll shoot you!'

'Look, bugger off, captain,' said the sergeant-major indifferently. 'I've seen enough of you nervous types. Your shooting can't be up to much, or the Germans wouldn't be so close to Moscow.'

'You skunk!' The captain went for his holster, but the squat little sergeant-major spat on the store-room floor in front of him and insolently turned his back, considering the conversation closed.

'Damn you,' said the captain with a sigh as he went out into the station yard. If you'd been under my command at the Dnieper! But then, they don't send your sort to the front, he thought, calming down a little. There was nothing for you to bawl about, you former political instructor (he said to himself). You used to be a man, but now you're just an appendage to the women ... Ah, to hell with him! The captain cooled down completely, and was glad that no one had heard the conversation in the store-room.

'Where can I pick up provisions? Any idea?' he asked his young driver after they had driven out through the gates.

'We'll find out,' replied the soldier. His voice was confident, and he had the clean, fine-featured face of a city-dweller. They did not have to look long for a supply-base.

As they were driving down a narrow, cobbled, steeply sloping street (having been released from hospital only the previous morning, and not knowing Moscow, the captain was not sure where exactly it was), an elderly man jumped out in front of their truck. He held up his arms and cried to them: 'Comrades! Comrades! Help! Thieves!'

'Bloody hell!' the driver swore as he jammed on the brakes and swerved sharply on to the pavement.

'They're looting, commander! They've carried off half the shop!'

'Where?' demanded the captain, making for his holster for the second time in about a quarter of an hour.

What was going on inside the little food shop was scarcely visible from the street, but it was packed like an unreserved train carriage. The only window had been smashed, and through it bags of grain and sugar were being passed. There was an incredible din, rather like a railway station.

The captain gave a gasp. He strode over, limping awkwardly on his wounded leg, and without thinking jabbed the butt of his pistol into the back of some fellow wearing a coat with a fur collar, who was in the act of receiving an unopened crate through the window.

Thank goodness it's not a woman, he thought, and immediately fired into the air.

'Stop this or I'll shoot!' he shouted, trembling as though he were shell-shocked.

Everyone in the shop shrank back from the window and froze, as if posing for a photograph. Only the fellow in the winter coat was still rummaging about for his cap, which had fallen on to the pavement.

The captain bore down on the shopkeeper: 'How did you let this happen? Why didn't you call the police? Or are you in cahoots with them?'

'Comrade Commander, what are you saying? I didn't throw anything away, or try and escape like the others . . .'

'You should have phoned.'

'We don't have a phone – it's just a small shop.'

'Well, this is a fine mess,' sighed the captain. 'Hey, you back there. Where d'you think you're going?' He pointed his pistol threateningly at a small boy who was about to jump out through the window. 'Can they escape through the back door?'

'No, it's padlocked,' said the shopkeeper, humbly.

'Well, you better run and phone, hadn't you? And get your finger out, will you? I'll give you two minutes.'

'Oh, thank you. Thank you for catching them all,' the old man whined as he crossed the road to a telephone box.

'It's out of order,' he shouted back. 'And this one, too,' he almost wept from the neighbouring one.

'Bloody hell!' the captain cursed. 'I don't have time to sunbathe with you. I've got women to feed. Listen, you don't happen to know where there's an army supply-base round here?'

'Oh, don't go away yet, Comrade Commander!' the breathless shopkeeper begged. 'Stay a minute longer – without you it will all start up again . . . Or go – go if you must. But shoot me first – I've had it now anyway!'

'Are you out of your mind? Where's the army supply-base?'

'What do you need a supply-base for, Comrade Officer? Is it provisions you need? Take them. Sugar? Take it. Butter? A box of it? Help yourself. Cereals? Take them! I don't hoard them for myself, you know – it's all for the war-effort. And they're stealing it! Take whatever you need, Commander: better that your wives and children are fed than this rabble!'

'What are you drivelling about? Wives? The Germans have got my wife and kids. You're crackers, old man . . . But wait a minute. I've got all the proper documents. Maybe you can supply me? I've got three hundred women and no grub for them.'

'Of course, of course!' the shopkeeper fussed. 'You lie where you are!' he snapped at the old man in the winter coat, who had at last found his cap and was trying to stand up from the pavement. 'You should be ashamed, Prokhor Stepanovich, an old man like you.'

'You know him?' asked the captain. 'Or are they all your friends? Listen, Comrade: you get them organized, they can load up the truck. What do you think, soldier?' He turned to the driver, who was slouched against the side of the truck, smoking unconcernedly.

'Quite right, Comrade Captain. Let them do some work!'

'Right, come out and start loading,' shouted the captain, feeling cheerier. 'I'll let you off this time – though you're lucky!'

'I suppose it would be better to leave it for the Germans?' asked the old man in the coat bitterly.

'What Germans?'

'What Germans? Ordinary ones. You should listen to the radio.'

'You watch your tongue. And start loading this truck before I change my mind,' said the captain angrily. 'A panic-monger, eh? Get working!'

He nodded to the shopkeeper: 'See to the papers, will you? I'll sign wherever I have to . . . What's all this about Germans coming? It's because of rogues like them that we're in retreat.'

'You should be shooting at the front, not here,' replied some woman from under a sack which she and two girls, apparently her daughters, were lifting. 'It wasn't our idea. The command was not to leave anything . . .'

'Oh yes?' The captain turned to the storekeeper. 'What else did the radio say?'

'I don't know. I didn't hear,' he replied. ' "There will be an important announcement shortly," they were saying. But I don't have a wireless here. Maybe it's nonsense. There's a lot of rumours about now.'

'It is nonsense,' said the captain firmly. 'Don't lose heart, old man! Thanks for the provisions. I'll head off straight for the trenches now – my women will be getting hungry!'

'And I thank you! Sign here, and here . . . I've given you the lot – two cases of butter and noodles, eight sacks containing millet, sugar and buckwheat . . .'

'It's all right, I believe you. Goodbye!' shouted the captain, already getting into the truck. 'See you after the victory!'

He turned to the driver and pulled out a map from under his greatcoat. 'Now, full speed ahead and to where the cross is marked. Do you see it?'

Three hundred women – he could not get them out of his head. One was bad enough, kept him awake at nights, but here he had three hundred! He could see his wife, Serafima, in front of him so clearly he could almost reach out and touch her. He was light and frail, but she was an imposing woman, twice his breadth and weight. She didn't half give me a 'political reprimand', he smiled to himself . . . Like all men who feel somewhat oppressed by their families, the former political instructor liked to whet his whistle occasionally . . . If the second battalion had known what punches Serafima could throw! Perhaps they did! Our soldiers are inquisitive lads – they find out about everything!

And you got about a bit, didn't you, political instructor? he said to himself. Or rather, you used to, when you were still an assistant platoon-commander. Once you became a political instructor, not so much – on manoeuvres once, a couple of times in the sanatorium. After that, nothing . . . Who are you trying to kid? he winked to himself. No, it's true. There wasn't any of that with Raisa . . .

Raisa was the matron of the military hospital. A very independent comrade, unmarried.

You could say, you went right to the edge, but resisted, the captain smiled again, recalling how she had embraced him the previous day in the linen-room, when he was changing back into his army clothes. She fancied me, that's certain. All the lads were looking for a chance to cuddle her, but I played it cool: always politely used the full form of her name, asked her how she was keeping, and so on . . . She liked that. But it's bad. Simka is probably rubbing soot in her cheeks now to make herself unattractive. Thank God she's not so young, at least (or so beautiful, you must admit!) . . . OK – he agreed with himself – she's not so beautiful, but beauty isn't everything. The lads she bore me, on the other hand, are top-notch! Ah! Forget it! You screw someone else's here; the Krauts are screwing yours over there . . .

He suddenly coughed, because the smell of burning wafted into the cabin. Something was being burned somewhere, it seemed, and a thick grey cloud, like snow, or the fluff from poplar trees, came floating along the street towards the truck.

What's wrong with you? – the captain interrupted himself. What are you going on about? Simka might not even be alive . . . The wife of a commander. Until last year the wife of a political instructor.

And he desperately longed for Serafima – or Simka – with all her faults. He longed to see that same Simka, the cook in the officers' mess, with whom he had gone out seven years earlier, without any thought of marriage. He married her out of kindness and pity, because Simka did not want to lose the child. The regimental commander had also pressed him: 'Marry her, Gavrilov. I don't want to transfer you from here. You're a born Red commander – a real Shchors,* apart from the beard. Marry her and be done with it! Her age' (Simka was six years his senior) 'is all to the good: she won't mess around in the garrison.'

'Are you married?' Gavrilov asked the driver. They had already left Moscow and passed two checkpoints, and were racing along an open road, almost empty.

'No.' The driver shook his head, without taking his cigarette out of his mouth.

He wouldn't understand, thought Gavrilov. And I don't have

* A hero of the Civil War [Tr.]

33

the words to explain how much I want to leave all this and go home to Simka. Home! What do you mean! He felt angry: this is home!

None the less he wanted home, where everything would be arranged according to Simka's tastes, like their first room together. They had no possessions, but Simka made everything homelike in no time. By evening she was calling in the officers for tea with jam. 'Gavrilov's lucky,' the unmarried officers would say enviously, as they scraped out their saucers of jam and hurried away to dance with the girls. Gavrilov would stand obediently at the stove or primus with a towel, drying the dishes while Simka washed up.

But now, when everything's topsy-turvy, and I'm growing old (thirty already; grey hairs), quite honestly, girls aren't the key to happiness. If Simka was sitting next to me, instead of this driver with his fag in his mouth, I'd be only half as afraid. She can even drive – I taught her. In general, she's a capable woman. She should have gone to an institute and became an industrial manager. In a steelworks. They say there's only one woman manager of a steelmill in the whole country. That's what Simka should have done . . .

And look what's cropped up now, he went on. I don't know how I'll cope without you. I've got all these women. Three hundred souls – like a landlord. I've never commanded women in my life before. I could do with you as an adviser – you'd put them in order in no time. My commands from the roof of the truck had no effect whatsoever . . .

Thinking about Serafima made him feel more comfortable. He raised his wounded leg and rested it against the side of the cabin.

'What's the road like?' he asked the driver. They had now turned off the main highway on to another road, also asphalted, but narrower.

'Not bad. No need to brake,' the driver nodded. And true enough, the road was even quieter than the other. There was no traffic in either direction. The only sound was the whistle of the wind, plus some very sporadic anti-aircraft fire somewhere in the distance.

'You're not scared of the bombing?' Gavrilov asked.

'No.'

'Perhaps we'll catch up on the women.'

'Quite likely,' agreed the driver.

So that's how things are, Simka – Gavrilov returned to his thoughts. But just then the tongue-tied driver blushed and asked suddenly in a brittle, boyish voice: 'Comrade Captain, permission to speak! Are you from this area?'

'No, I've been in various places,' Gavrilov yawned.

'You see, I wanted to ask . . . But don't think I'm panicking.'

'Go ahead, ask me.'

What's this, Simka, he thought. He's nervous about something. 'Spit it out!' he said to the driver.

'You see, I'm from Moscow. Or at least, I'm from Kharkov, but I've been here two years. I was called up after my first visit as a student. But you know, there's never been a message like that before – "There will be an important announcement shortly." '

'So?'

'When the war broke out it was: "We are broadcasting over all the radio stations of the Soviet Union." '

'I don't get your question,' said Gavrilov. 'You've been a student for a whole year, yet you don't understand the situation. What do you think the situation is?'

'The Germans are approaching Moscow.'

'That's not the situation, it's just a detail,' said Gavrilov, pulling a face. 'You haven't grasped the essential point. And that, if you want to know a secret, is not to think too hard and carry out orders. You've got a good empty road ahead of you – step on it and be glad you can go so fast. As for me, I'm glad I've got top-quality food for the women, and not rotten synthetic lard. If you try to solve everyone else's problems, you'll have no strength left for your own responsibilities and duties. Stalin's defending Moscow; you're driving a truck. Clear?'

'That's clear, all right, Comrade Captain. But, you know what I mean, the road's very quiet . . .'

'That's not your problem. What are you, a road inspector?'

We've got a brainy one here, Simka, Gavrilov addressed his wife. Straight from college! But he's right – the road is deserted. What if they . . .

'Ah, shit!' he swore out loud, and jerked as though he had been punched on the jaw.

'Toothache, Comrade Captain?' asked the driver.

'Uh-huh,' nodded Gavrilov, who only ever saw dentists at medical inspections.

'Have a cigarette. It'll help.'

'I can't. I've got a bullet-wound in my lung,' said the captain truthfully.

'How did that happen?' The driver, who still had not seen action, blushed.

'Machine-gun fire, from a tank. My nerves broke down and I rushed forward . . . But to hell with it – that's the least of my worries, lad. My wife and kids are in occupied territory.'

'Yes, I heard. You were telling the shopkeeper.'

'That's the worst thing, soldier.'

'Yes, I understand.'

'I don't suppose you really do, but thanks for the sympathy.'

This road could be on another planet: there's not a soul, he thought, but said aloud: 'You know yourself: the reserves aren't stationed here. They're in some secret place.'

'We'll thrash the Germans here, like Napoleon,' rejoined the student confidently.

'We thrashed Napoleon after he entered Moscow. Adolf will cop it before Moscow,' Gavrilov corrected him.

'They say the Americans are landing at Mytishchi.* Is that true?'

'No. There are a lot of rumours about just now. You shouldn't believe them all. America hasn't declared war on the Krauts.'

'Perhaps it's the British?' asked the driver hopefully.

'What about the Dutch – you haven't mentioned them! We mustn't count on anyone except ourselves,' said the captain firmly. 'Rely on us. There are a lot of us. And so what if the road's empty: it doesn't matter.'

'Of course not,' nodded the student. 'It's good, in fact. We can go faster. We'll soon catch up on the train, and be on our way back!'

He's catching on! thought the captain, but aloud he said: 'What do you mean, "We'll be on our way back"? There will be a fortification commander on the spot, and he'll tell us what to do. And you'll turn this truck round if and when I give the order. Do you understand?'

But realizing that he had been excessively rude and that there was no need for extremes with this driver, Gavrilov put his hand on his shoulder, as if to say: 'Don't worry, lad, we'll be all right!' or something like that.

* Just north of Moscow. [Tr.]

'The fortification engineer will know what's what,' said the captain, and added, uncertainly, knowing he was making it up: 'They've got telephone communications, or even radio. They probably heard this "important announcement" yesterday. Assuming it's not a cock-and-bull story,' he added, to reassure himself. 'No, they won't surrender Moscow. Moscow's a question of politics, mate. Moscow, even though you and I aren't from there, is everything. We even use the word "Moscow" to mean any huge number of people.'

'Yes,' the driver grinned. 'You also say "Moscow" when you get two aces instead of one. It means you're bust!'

'Don't you get witty with me!' The captain frowned. 'Moscow may be "bust" at cards, but not in real life.'

6

Moscow may not have been bust, but things did not turn out quite right. At a level-crossing the empty, vari-coloured train, with the engine at the back, raced past them in the direction of Moscow, and as soon as it was gone they could see the women crossing the potato field with their buckets.

'Will I drive to the church, Comrade Captain?' asked the driver.

'Yes. We should be able to find . . .'

But they never did find the fortification engineer.

'There was no one like that here,' said the old man in the trenchcoat, politely, as though apologizing, and spread his hands. 'There have been no detachments here for two days. Perhaps they passed through during the night?'

'Did you hear shooting?'

'I'm afraid I'm a little hard of hearing,' said the old man in an embarrassed tone. 'And my youngsters,' he pointed to the boys pottering about nearby, 'sleep like logs. But they probably are shooting. Only far away. The windows in our house ring ever so slightly, and the crockery in the sideboard sometimes makes a tiny moaning sound, as though it were sad,' he added, not sure whether to be pleased with his poetic simile or to apologize for it.

'That's clear,' said the captain, though there was nothing clear about it.

'Excuse me, are these your, how shall I put it, soldiers?' asked the old man, pointing to the women strung out across the field.

'Yes, they're going to be digging trenches,' replied Gavrilov. 'Get in the truck!' he said angrily to his driver, regretting not having sent him away earlier; now he had heard their conversation. Still, you can't hide the truth, he thought.

'Hey, group-leader,' he shouted to Ganya's 'commander', Maria Ivanovna, as she clambered on to the road. She was as big as his wife, Simka, and he remembered her from the morning. 'I've brought food for you – first-class stuff. Tell your girls to unload it.'

'Yes, sir!' she called, and went over to the truck.

'Help them,' Gavrilov said to the driver.

The women set to the task, but not so briskly as in the morning, when the tools arrived. The trek across the field seemed to have worn them out.

'I'll have to billet them somewhere,' said Gavrilov, turning back to the old man, who was respectfully awaiting further orders. 'Is there a village nearby?'

'It's about two kilometres away.'

'That's no good. Trench-digging's no game. What's in the church? A repair-shop? They can sleep there, then. And you, er . . .'

'Of course, of course,' the old man fussed. 'We understand. Everything for the war-effort. We want to contribute too. The defences here will turn out marvellously.'

Thank goodness they're staying here, thought the old man joyfully. Where could Klavdia and I retreat to? I'll fix up a corner in the cellar for her in case there's shooting. The poor soul mustn't get upset . . . And be began to expound the virtues of river-defence to Gavrilov.

'All right. So long as it's a professional job,' said the captain.

'Lads!' the old man shouted, like the colonel at the Battle of Borodino, almost adding: 'Is not Moscow behind us?!' 'Hurry up with those cylinders. We've got real work for you to do: cutting rails and welding anti-tank barriers.'

'Listen, old man!' The captain called after him. 'Excuse me, I don't know your name. Mikhail Fyodorich? You're obviously a sensible, experienced man. An engineer, I suppose. So in the meantime I'm putting you in charge of the fortifications here.'

'Well, actually, it was just the Samara Technical Institute I was at – with Sergei Kirov – much earlier, I mean,' the old man stammered nervously. 'But I did graduate, I did graduate,' he added. 'So I'm not exactly a full engineer, and it was a different subject . . . but I'll take it on, certainly, I'll take it on . . . It's just the women I'm a little afraid of . . .'

'It's all right. They've got their own commanders. You just draw a plan of where they've to dig, and leave them to it.'

'I mustn't dampen people's enthusiasm, he said to himself. 'I'm sure they'll make a go of it,' he added aloud. 'And one other thing, Mikhail Fyodorich, show the driver where the nearest telegraph office is.'

He tossed the map-case to the driver: 'Catch!'

'Listen,' he said, going up to Maria Fyodorovna, who was supervising the unloading. 'You keep order here while I'm gone. Let them make porridge. Use plenty of butter – feed them well. They'll be sleeping in the church – send them for hay and straw or bedding, or they'll all catch cold.'

'Yes, sir,' she laughed. 'Understood! Off you go!' She winked meaningfully.

'Yes. And don't overwork them – only until it gets dark, no longer.'

'We can light fires for extra light,' put in Mikhail Fyodorich.

'There'll be no fires!' the captain cut him off touchily. What have I done to deserve so many activists today, he wondered, and explained: 'I think we've had enough planes for one day.'

'I thought it was a matter of extreme urgency . . .'

'It requires some common sense, too,' barked Gavrilov, but immediately had second thoughts and patted the old man's shoulder, as he had the driver's earlier, as if to say: it's not for me to teach you things, Mikhail Fyodorich, but we are in an extraordinary situation.

What if communications are severed? he wondered. How am I going to get them out of here when they're all exhausted from digging? It's like this all the time: some of them you have to urge on, others (these activists!) you have to hold back – and you've no strength left for the Germans!

'Let's find this post office,' he said to the driver.

It was dark in the church because nearly all the windows were boarded up. There was a smell of hot iron and oil from a broken motor, but Liya was delighted by these unfamiliar smells. She slipped through the door – which was wide enough for a tractor – sideways, as if it were just a crack.

'Will we pray?!' She heard laughter behind her back.

'Oh, it's ages since I was in a church.'

'This isn't a church – it's a rubbish dump,' complained an older voice.

'Liya, keep them away from me,' Ganya whispered, but she was immediately assailed by the women.

'You're not wearing a cross!'

'The Lord will remember!'

'He doesn't exist!' Ganya mocked. Her face was like a mischievous cat's. 'As for my cross, I traded it in at the shop for foreigners.'

That's awful, thought Liya. After all, there may not be many of them, but there are still religious people, and it's insulting to them. You have to respect others' feelings. True, this is just a workshop now, but how terribly boorish we still are . . . And she reddened at the memory of how Sanka's father, the house-manager, had burst into her room the day before war broke out to claim her 'extra' space . . . 'Sanka's moving in here. What do you need a huge room like this for?' he bawled, drunkenly, and suddenly started embracing her, pouting his lips inanely. Liya squirmed with disgust and backed away into the room, afraid to push a drunk and elderly man. But just then Sanka flew in from the corridor and thumped her father on the back for all she was worth. Then she and Liya cried the night away, with their arms around each other.

Suddenly the squad-leaders' voices echoed round the church: 'Stop snoozing in there!'

'To work, ladies!'

'Come out and get stuck into it!'

In front of the church the tubby little round-faced old man was waving his arms about, directing the women to their places.

'On the other side of that hill, at the foot of the slope, dig one-man trenches – no less than thirty paces apart – and stagger them so they won't be shooting each other in the necks. On the hillside itself dig ditches about fifty yards long, and to about shoulder-height: together with the parapet, that should be about right. And make them winding. Let me show you!'

He asked Ganya for her spade and ran to mark out the line of a trench on the hillside.

'The old fellow can't sit still,' said Ganya in amazement.

And true enough, Mikhail Fyodorich was buzzing about like a bee. For the first time in his sixty-odd years, the village maths and physics teacher (and seasonal technician at the Tractor Station) had the opportunity to command nearly a whole battalion. Until now his fame had been confined to a radius of less than three miles, and to a set of children who listened with ever-dwindling patience to his joyful babbling about bodies immersed in liquid, and roots and squares. And just when he had begun to lose hope, good fortune fell out of the sky, and he became truly necessary. And what a stroke of luck that it should have happened right on his doorstep, so that all the neighbours could see him – Mikhail Fyodorich, an elderly but active and thoughtful chap, by his own example and personal leadership, keeping the enemy from Moscow.

'What are you catching flies for?' The boss pounced on Ganya. 'Where's your spade?'

'The old man's borrowed it! Maria Ivanovna . . . I'd be better fetching buckets of water – I'll do it in a jiffy, I'll . . .'

'Oh no you don't. They'll manage without you. Go and get another spade and start digging!'

And Ganya trudged towards the hill, enviously looking over her shoulder at the women by the church. Some were bringing water from the river, others were pottering about, arranging smoke-blackened buckets over the fires, while others still lugged sacks of provisions into the church in case it should rain. Two women who had found axes in the repair-shop were mercilessly attacking the wooden shed in the churchyard.

'Take it easy, girls!' Maria Ivanovna shouted to them. 'Leave the captain a corner somewhere. Otherwise he'll have to spend the night with you in the church, and that wouldn't be decent, would it?'

'Ha!' replied the girls, and their laughter was echoed by the cooks at the camp-fire. Everyone was in fighting spirits. Maria Ivanovna went to see how the trenches were coming along.

'Digging, eh? Well done,' she praised Ganya. 'Your porridge won't run away – there's plenty for everyone. The captain managed to get real butter, too.' Then she spotted Liya. 'Look at the way you're holding that spade! What a weakling you are –

spent too much time reading books. Look at Ganya – that's how to go about it! Well done, Beaky,' she nodded to Ganya. 'Double portions for you! And you learn, Ginger! What are these queer boots you've got on? You should chop the heels off, they're getting in the way.'

'She'll get better,' said Sanka quietly, embarrassed for her friend. But the chief did not hear and moved off down the line of diggers.

Right along the hilly riverbank, from bridge to bridge, the women excavated the ground. It was hard to think that these were the same women who before dawn had turned away from the picks and crowbars and jostled in the queue for spades. Now, with the train journey and the trek across the potato field behind them, they were infected by a kind of cheerful serenity, and were annoyed only by the darkness creeping over the grey sky, consuming the road beyond the bridge and the forest on the horizon.

'Come on!'

'We've a long way to go.'

'It's getting dark. Get your backs into it!'

'Pretend you're digging Jerry a grave.'

'He won't get this far!' came voices all along the bank.

We're like ants, thought Ganya, resting for a moment and surveying the hillside.

'Come on, Liya, attack the ground! she shouted suddenly to the red-haired girl. Having earned the boss's praise, Ganya instinctively regarded herself as 'above' the others and felt she could shout at her comrades. There was no need: they were all making an effort. At the top of the hill, which looked stony, four women raised their picks in unison.

The young volunteer Goshka sang to himself:

> An iron spade
> Against a stormy chest . . .

At the foot of the hill, almost opposite the road bridge, he was standing up to the hem of his short coat in the clayey one-man trench he was digging.

'Are you digging one for yourself?' Sanka shouted down to him.

'Uh-huh!' he said dismissively, hurling away a spadeful of yellow earth, Sanka had interrupted his thoughts. He had been imagining Karina watching him from the hillside, and under her reassuring gaze the boy felt like a veteran of three wars. He was indeed digging for himself. This is where I'll stay! he daydreamed. If only I had a rifle, or – better – a Degtyaryov machine-gun. Rat-ta-ta-ta . . .! He knelt down on one knee and took aim with his imaginary machine-gun at the trees on the opposite bank.

In the meantime Maria Ivanovna had satisfied herself that everything was in order. As she strode past the tubby old man, he tried to explain to her how he intended to secure the defences.

'Well, good luck,' she yawned, cutting off – as graciously as possible – his prattle, which was too abstruse and too well-mannered for her taste. 'I must check how the girls are getting on.'

Yes, the work's going well, she reflected, I didn't need to be armed after all . . .! I just hope *he* doesn't slip away, the bugger! She suddenly remembered the thin, unhappy-looking Captain Gavrilov . . . No, he wouldn't – he's a conscientious type. Brought us decent food! And, smiling about something, she floated off towards the church.

Here the fires were blazing and sparking, and a couple of dozen buckets were bubbling with food.

'Have a taste!' the farthest-away cook called to Maria Ivanovna. 'How are we doing? The quality's probably not up to much, but there's plenty of it!'

'Well done,' Maria Ivanovna replied cheerfully, taking the ladle and raising it ceremoniously to her lips, as though it contained vodka, not porridge.

'Seems to have the right amount of salt,' she said, rather than praise them, so as not to lose her dignity as a commander. 'I'll go and round up the girls. Don't put the fires out completely – leave some hot food for the captain.'

7

Gavrilov and the driver were bumping along a shattered stone road, on to which they had turned immediately behind the railway bridge. The student, to Gavrilov's delight, was silent, constantly consulting the map and worrying lest he miss the next turn-off. It was fast growing dark.

'How many women could you take in the truck?' asked Gavrilov all of a sudden.

'About twenty-five, if they kept still. Why?'

'No reason.'

At twenty-five a time, that would make twelve journeys, thought Gavrilov. Say thirteen, including the provisions and all the equipment. Now, if I were to move them about twenty kilometres, that would make . . . thirteen times twenty . . . two hundred and sixty – double that for the return trips. A day and a half's work . . .

'It won't work, Comrade Captain. There's not enough petrol,' said the driver, who had apparently been doing the same sums.

'I know. Watch you don't miss the turn-off,' said Gavrilov gloomily. 'Is it close?'

'Just coming up. I'll get the sick and the old out . . .' The student wanted to have the last word.

'OK, we'll see,' Gavrilov snapped. Playing the bloody activist again, he thought, wearily.

Meanwhile the truck had entered the village. It was now quite dark. There was no light in the windows of the wooden houses, either because they were blacked out or because there was no electricity or kerosene.

'Bloody hell,' the captain swore. 'Where the devil is this post office? Try knocking at the first door, will you?'

'We can follow the telegraph wires,' said the student, unable to conceal his pleasure at his own quick-wittedness. 'There it is!' he exclaimed triumphantly, pulling up outside a crooked little hut whose windows were also unlit.

'Fine!' sighed the captain as he climbed out of the cabin, limping again on his injured leg. 'Bah! It's locked!' he cried from the porch. 'Damn them!'

He hammered on the door but no one answered.

'What's wrong with 'em, have they snuffed out? Try the neighbours, student.'

'Who's there?' said an old woman's voice in the darkness.

'Where's the telegraph-operator?'

'Where d'you think she is, you goats?! Think she works all night? Drive out to the edge of the village – hers is the third house from the end.'

44

'Thank you,' the student replied for the captain.

'That's a fine bloody state of affairs,' said Gavrilov with a grim smile as he climbed into the truck. 'It's like the stone age.'

'Exactly,' the student agreed.

The captain barged into the third house from the end without knocking. The room was dimly lit by an oil-lamp. At the table opposite the door sat a thin old man with an untidy beard and a bald dome of a head. He appeared to be tipsy, because there was an empty bottle in front of him, and, having discarded his spoon, he was scooping up great handfuls of *sauerkraut* from his plate.

'You're not the flamin' telegraphist, are you?' bawled Gavrilov.

'Naw!' The old man shook his dome, which gleamed in the dim lamplight like a smooth old door-knob.

'That's her over there!' He jabbed his finger, covered with *sauerkraut*, in the direction of a woman, who (as Gavrilov could now make out) was sitting in a corner wearing a coat and shawl, with a pair of glasses on her long nose.

'Give her her orders, soldier! Tell her to give her father some decent grub! I know she hides it all from me at that post office of hers, damn that bloody post . . .'

'Let's go,' said Gavrilov to the woman. 'I need to make a call.'

'We'll all go,' the old man exclaimed gleefully and tried to get up from the table. 'Now we'll sniff out her little store! Let's have a drink, soldier!'

'Lock him in,' said the captain with a look of disgust as he stepped out into the dark street.

'There's no need,' replied the woman, 'he won't go further than the door. Mind where you walk, officer; they dug holes for new telegraph poles here in the spring . . .'

'Follow on with the truck!' Gavrilov shouted into the darkness. 'Does your father always drink so much?' he added, allowing the woman to walk in front.

'Oh, it's terrible, officer. We buried my step-mother on Sunday: he hasn't been sober since.'

'I see,' Gavrilov sighed. Some people have enough to worry about without the war, he thought. It's only when you leave the main road that you see it!

'Will they connect us with Moscow immediately?' he asked, climbing the steps to the post office behind the woman.

'I'll try.' She groped for a key under the railing and fumbled about with the padlock. 'Hold on, I'll get some light.'

There was no electricity here either, but a paraffin lamp allowed Gavrilov to make out the room and the woman. They were in an ordinary-looking office with a low partition, behind which stood a table with a field telephone, a trestle-bed covered with a grey blanket, a filing cabinet, and beside it a stove – a Dutch one, not Russian. The telegraph-operator was fairly young, but plain and rather scrawny, and dominated by her spectacles. For a moment Gavrilov was touched with pity: Even without the war you'd have ended up an old maid, and now . . . But time was too short for such sentiments, and, unbuttoning the pocket of his field-shirt under his greatcoat, he handed the girl a piece of paper with a number on it. The telephone worked from a dry battery, and calls were put through by turning a handle. But even the sight of this antediluvian equipment restored the captain's confidence, and when the girl – after countless interjections and exclamations (Hello! Waiting! Go ahead! Hello, dear!) – handed him the warm receiver, he firmly believed that everything would work out, that the enemy would be routed and Soviet power would triumph.

The receiver crackled unrelentingly, and Moscow sounded light-years away, but none the less at the othe end of the line could be sensed the calm orderliness of the capital, and straining his voice, coughing and spitting, Gavrilov shouted: 'Who is speaking? Who? I can't hear you? This is Gavrilov . . . Captain Gavrilov here . . .'

Suddenly a voice burst through the crackling: 'I hear you. Where are speaking from? Where . . .? Ah, I see. What do you want?' asked a sleepy voice.

'Tozhanov. Comrade Tozhanov.'

'Tozhanov's not here.'

'Comrade, don't hang up. I've got three hundred women . . . the ones sent to dig trenches. But there are no engineers here – not a single one.'

'I see.' The voice at the other end became firmer. 'So what on earth did you take them there for . . .' They were sent? And there was no commander there . . .? You should have sent them back by train . . . There wasn't one? Have you got provisions? Fruit and vegetables . . . Hang on a minute, I'll find out . . .'

For about five minutes the line just crackled. Gavrilov was in a sweat.

'Sit down, Comrade Captain,' said the girl. 'Would you like me to pour you something?'

'No.' He shook his head, with the receiver still at his ear, and with his free hand pressed the girl's hand on the back of the chair. Her hand was rough and work-worn, but warm, and human.

'Sit down,' she said, even more quietly.

'Hey, Gavrilov, are you there?' Again a voice broke through the crackles. 'What's the situation? Digging? Quite right, keep digging! Here? What do you mean? – everything's under control. An important announcement? What announcement? Ah, that . . . No, there hasn't been one. But there will be – soon, don't worry. You'll hear about it. So listen here: they'll send goods-vans for you. Or else engineers, depending on the situation. I phoned them – they promised . . . Expect them,' the voice faltered, 'around fifteen, no, better make that sixteen hours. Meanwhile, keep digging. Make sure they're deep enough! Wait until sixteen hours. Then send them off on foot. They're not children, they'll make it. Understand?'

'Yes, sir! Sixteen hours, understood!' Gavrilov shouted joyfully into the mouthpiece, forgetting to ask whom he had been speaking with.

'May I pour you a drink, Comrade Captain?' asked the telephonist once more.

'You may, you may!' Gavrilov exclaimed, and, being unable to embrace the man at the other end of the line, he hugged the telephonist and kissed her on the face beside her glasses, still holding on to the telephone receiver. 'You certainly may, my dear! How much do I owe you for the call? Will ten do?' He let the girl go and felt for his field-shirt pocket under his coat.

'Never mind, I'll let you off,' said the embarrassed girl. 'Oh, you're . . .'

'What am I?' he asked, holding out the money.

'Serious – that's what,' she replied uncertainly. 'Here, I'll get your drink.' She took a bottle and a cut-glass tumbler from the filing cabinet. 'Shall I write out a receipt for you?' she asked in a gently mocking tone.

'Yes, write one out, dear,' he said with a sigh, suddenly forgetting her and seeing before his eyes only the women scraping at the ground near the village church. 'Better do everything according to the book,' he added aloud, though he was already thinking about the return trip. 'Let's drink, then . . . What am I playing at? – Hey, student!' he shouted, throwing open the door of the post office. 'Come here! Are you frozen?' He pushed the brimming glass into the driver's hand as soon as he had stumbled into the room, timidly pulling off his forage cap. 'Drink it! You have my permission. I'll drive back.'

'Thank you,' said the driver with a nod.

'Three roubles eighty kopecks,' said the girl.

'Keep the change: buy yourself some perfume!' shouted Gavrilov, and ran down from the porch, forgetting in his joy to pick up the receipt.

The women had found neither straw nor hay. The shrewdest of them took over the sacristy, which was low-ceilinged and less draughty. There was enough tarpaulin – taken from the provisions – to cover about two dozen of the women for the night. The others – not far short of three hundred – covered the church floor from the iconostasis to the vestibule. They spread coats and wadded jackets underneath and around themselves, and huddled closely so as not to freeze altogether.

'Never mind, soldiers! The captain will get us hay for tomorrow!'

'We'll manage army-style for one night!'

'Kasha* and Masha will keep us warm!'

'Take off that quilted jacket – share and share alike!' The vaulted ceiling echoed with voices.

'I just hope there are no mice.'

'What, would you rather have rats?!'

'I'd rather have that driver . . .'

'The captain would be all right.'

'The captain's for Maria Ivanovna!'

'Ah yes, the bosses should keep each other warm . . .'

'Quiet, over there!' Maria Ivanovna responded with pleasure. 'Instead of wagging your tongues so much, you could take in that young lad.' She nodded towards Goshka, who was standing at the door, not knowing where to go.

Maybe the truck will come back and I can chat with the captain or the soldier, he was thinking. What am I supposed to do among all these women?

* Porridge [Tr.]

48

'Come over here, Goshka,' cried Sanka. She was lying against the right wall, with Liya and Ganya close by.

Goshka muttered something and went out to the porch.

It was pitch-dark, but high above the church, where the wind had thinned out the clouds, a few stars were blinking. Moscow was far away. And his aunt, his father's unmarried sister, who had raised him and nagged him in lieu of his parents, who were Arctic explorers, was also far away. And because Karina, too, was far away – somewhere on the road to Kazan or Gorky, he supposed – he felt sad, but at the same time free, and he experienced a soldier's anxiety and joy. It was as spacious, looking out from the church, as it was from his Moscow rooftop, but much more out of the ordinary and so a hundred times better. And there was more scope for his imagination. The noise in the church was dying down, and the sparking of the wood smouldering in the fires also grew less, and inspired his dreams like soft music. Warmed inside by two bowls of porridge, Goshka felt himself melting away, growing lighter and at the same time bigger, like a huge cloud growing out of the ground, until he felt as huge as the church, and able – alone and unarmed – to guard the bridge and the riverbank. And Karina, now en route to Kazan, was just a tiny speck, and he no longer regretted that he had merely shaken her hand at their farewell, and not embraced or kissed her, for how could be – such a giant – kiss a fifteen-year-old girl?

'Hey, lad! Fancy a baked potato?' a woman's voice called out.

'Uh?' Goshka started, and his dream faded, though something of it remained in him. He answered in a deeper, controlled voice: 'Yes, please,' and strode with an air of importance over to the camp-fire. After all, the cooks were a worthier lot than the other women, and it wasn't so shameful to sit with them in the dark, eating potatoes, while the others all slept.

'Here, dip your potato in this,' said one of the cooks, moving a bowl of melted butter towards him.

He did not look closely at their faces. They were just women, although they might just as well have been Red Army men: he was returning to his dream, although it was different now. He saw himself in a greatcoat, breeches and tarpaulin boots, no longer a giant, but filled with strength. Beside him lay an invisible rifle – an eight-millimetre (the most reliable to handle, not like the self-loaders – they caused no end of trouble in sandy places) and he

49

burned his fingers peeling his potato. The next day provisions might not be delivered, the whole detachment could be cut off at the bridge, and nobody might be able to get through to them for three days . . . but the Whites, that is, the Germans, would perish here in droves . . .

'Your potato all right?' asked the woman who had offered Goshka the butter. 'Good, aren't they? Let's take a bucketful into the church – the girls need warming up.'

'Where are you taking that? Who gave the order?' snorted Maria Ivanovna from the doorway. She was sitting on a stool near a lathe, waiting for the captain.

'Come on, love, we're takin' in some heat!' said the cook with a laugh.

'You're just waking people up,' the boss grumbled, but did not quash their initiative.

Sanka called to her: 'Cheer up, Maria Ivanovna. Come and lie with us. The captain's probably got stuck to the telephonist!'

'Don't,' Liya whispered quietly. She had not lain down yet and was squatting with her coat over her shoulders.

'Let's have a bit of your coat,' said Ganya, who was just finishing her porridge. She was the only one in the whole detachment without a bowl, and was therefore last to receive her portion. 'Thanks for the loan!' she said as she handed back Liya's sticky bowl and spoon.

'You could've washed it, slut,' commented Sanka, screwing up her face in disgust.

'It's all right. She's young – she can nip down to the river with it,' replied Ganya. She had sensed by now that Liya was weaker than the others and could easily be taken advantage of.

'Ooh, she can just "nip down",' Sanka mocked, imitating Ganya's voice.

'What's up with you? Does your man pamper you like that?' asked a woman lying nearby. There were only two lanterns for the whole church – one on the work-bench, the other on a lathe – and through the dark and the clouds of breath in the cold air Ganya could not see the woman.

'That's right,' she was about to answer, but Sanka got there first: 'She's never had a man. Just hangs around with other women's men.'

'What do you know about it?' Ganya exploded. 'Other women's! I've had my day, you know.'

'Once upon a time,' retorted Sanka.

'I went to Yessentuki with him . . .' Ganya continued, but suddenly burst into tears and turned away from Sanka.

No, she had not always 'hung around'. She had had her day. right at the beginning of the New Economic Policy, in Lipetsk, she and her mother and sister had baked pies and sold them at the railway station. And it was true that she had gone to Yessentuki with her young man, Sergei Yeryomich, who worked as a cabbie in Moscow, and her little sister, Klanka, who was still just a girl. And there, in the Caucasian spa, either in drunkenness or stupidity, Seryoga had got Klanka pregnant, and she was too afraid to get rid of it. She ran away from home and came back only when she was about to give birth. And she produced two nephews for Ganya. Then Seryoga appeared back in Lipetsk and announced he was taking Klanka off to near Moscow, where he had bought a house.

'How on earth will Klanka manage on her own?' asked her mother, who was now virtually confined to her bed.

'We'll take Ganya,' said Seryoga brusquely.

'But what about me?' asked Mother.

'You'll die alone,' Seryoga replied shamelessly, and Ganya left with her sister and nephews.

Seryoga had not been lying: he had bought a house of sorts, on the Iksha river outside of Moscow, and had even added to it. It wasn't so bad there. No worse than in Lipetsk. Now Ganya and Klanka took it in turns to sell pies at Savelovsky Station in Moscow. But without their mother's special pastry the business never got off the ground, and Seryoga had no intention of inviting a sick old woman to live with them.

And so their life continued – until Seryoga sold (or drank away!) his horse, learned to drive a lorry, and set off to earn 'big money' in more distant parts, and started appearing at the house on the Iksha only once in a couple of years, if that.

That was how it was . . . and Ganya could have told the whole story, but what was the point: the girls would not have understood, and anyway it was getting late. Half the church was sleeping and snoring, and those who were awake were chatting quietly: 'Go to sleep!'

'You'll be exhausted tomorrow.'

'All clear!' a voice rang out from a far corner. It was probably one of the girl students who had been singing the songs about the dove and 'the city we love' in the open goods-van during the air-raid that morning.

'Shhh! That sounds like a truck coming!' said Maria Ivanovna loudly and got up from her stool.

8

Five minutes later the captain and the student were sitting in the dark truck tucking into bowls of porridge, still perfectly warm.

'Well, how are my cooks?' asked Maria Ivanovna ostentatiously. 'You forgot to bring tea, captain, so I donated some of mine.'

'Thanks,' said Gavrilov sombrely. He could feel that the squad-leader was interested in him, and felt embarrassed for the student – and anyway it was not the time for such things.

'Second helpings?' asked Maria Ivanovna.

'Not for me,' said the captain, 'but give the driver some more – he needs it.' He nudged the student with his elbow, hinting either at the long drive or the glass of vodka.

'Yes, please, if there's some left,' said the student.

'There's loads left!' replied the 'commander' and disappeared into the church.

'Bedtime, lad, quick march!' she hissed at the young boy, who was still smoking in the doorway.

'I'm just going,' Goshka muttered in reply.

It was not as if he could not sleep, but he did not feel like it. And he still wanted to talk with the captain, or at least the driver. His dream had come so close – he would be a fool to let it go. He felt that in the quiet of the night, among three hundred women, three men (the fourth, the old 'engineer' had gone home to his wife in the village) would find it easier to come to some agreement, and they would not make fun of him as they had at the recruitment office the day before yesterday.

'Here's some nice hot tea. Mind you don't burn your fingers!' said Maria Ivanovna, returning with two mugs and a bowl of porridge. 'Eat up, soldier, and then get some sleep,' she said as she gave the student the bowl.

You've got it all planned out, thought Gavrilov. What is it about me that attracts these women commanders? Do they detect some weakness or other?

'Thanks again,' he said, handing back his mug and getting out of the cabin to stretch his numb shoulders.

'The soldier will sleep in the cabin,' whispered the 'commander', taking Gavrilov by the arm. 'And you'd feel out of place in the church, so I've reserved a corner in the shed for you. I'm afraid the girls got all the tarpaulins, but it's not so damp there: there's a wooden floor.'

'Go and join the girls, Maria Ivanovna. We're too old, you and I,' Gavrilov replied, also quietly, recalling his telephone conversation which no longer seemed so cheering to him.

'Oh-ho, you don't say!' The woman embraced him, playfully taking offence. Is he acting proud, or shy? she wondered. Policemen are different: they never get flustered. Not giving in, she added a loud: 'Old? How dare you?! I'm thirty-one. And you can't be much more?'

'Same age,' said Gavrilov, giving himself an extra year.

'You look too serious for that. But it's still not old – you're in your prime, captain, I'm telling you.'

'I'm wounded.' He decided to put a stop to this unnecessary conversation and ward her off – but in a way that would not offend her, since he had another whole day, or perhaps longer, to work with her.

'Oh, dear!' she whistled. 'Are you married?'

'Yes,' he barked, and thought angrily: She doesn't half cling to you, this one.

The squad-leader now gave voice to her thoughts, not sparing Gavrilov: 'You certainly give a woman a hard time.'

'Looks like it. Go and sleep, Maria Ivanovna.'

'Sleep well, poor devil,' she tossed at him as she climbed the broken steps to the church. Seeing Goshka, she vented her annoyance on him: 'Sleep! I've told you once!'

'What are you burning the midnight oil for?' she asked Liya and Sanka inside. 'Lie down, Fatty. I'll squeeze up beside you. It's dreadful, you know, how people get crippled!' she sighed, settling down between Ganya and Sanka. Ganya was already snoring.

'It's ridiculous, girls,' continued Maria Ivanovna, not waiting for a response, but dying to divulge her news.

'Oho!' Sanka almost burst out laughing.

'That's awful,' thought Liya, and a feeling of ill will towards her friend returned to her, together with the recollection of Sanka's father, the house-manager.

Liya stood up from the floor and made her way carefully past the sleeping bodies towards the door.

'Where are you going? Lie down!' Sanka hissed.

'Leave her! She's no hot-water bottle,' yawned the commander, snuggling into Sanka's pudgy back. 'Ah, well, that's the way of it,' she yawned again, and fell asleep.

Outside the wind had got up, and the roofing iron jingled in an almost devilish way. Gavrilov was swinging his arms quickly, as though at a keep-fit class, and every time he threw his head back another sprinkling of stars seemed to appear in the sky.

'Are you thinking about the bombing, Comrade Captain?' asked Goshka, who had not yet gone off to sleep, in a loud voice.

'Bloody h– . . .' Gavrilov stopped halfway through his usual oath because just at that moment some woman came out of the church. 'Well,' he asked a moment later, once the woman had gone round the back of the church, 'have you welded up a lot of barriers?'

'No, I'm not one of the local lads. I've been digging trenches.'

'Have you been attached to the women?'

'Yes. I asked to go to the front, but they sent me here,' complained Goshka, trying to elicit sympathy.

'Well, let's go and have a look at what you've dug,' said Gavrilov, guessing what was coming next. He'd have asked for the front line himself, rather than his present work, had his lung not been shot through.

'Hey, student! You keep guard for half an hour!' he shouted through the darkness to the driver. 'I'm going to take a look around . . .'

He nodded to Goshka: 'Let's go.'

Behind the church the wind was even stronger. Blowing from the river, it whistled through the church and carried off the women's snoring in the direction of the capital. All that could be heard on the hillside was the wind and the ringing iron.

What a lad, thought Gavrilov. Fourteen, and already scheming to get to the front. I'm glad my lads are younger . . . During the last four months he had asked himself perhaps a thousand times: was it good or bad that his boys were only six and three years old. Sometimes he thought that if they were older they would be less trouble for his wife, but at other times, on the contrary, he wished they were still tiny infants: the Germans would be less likely to touch them, or his wife. But now, watching Goshka from behind, Gavrilov considered that all in all he was lucky with his boys. They don't smoke, thank heavens, and they won't run off to the army, either, he consoled himself, forgetting that, at thirty, he could not in any case have children of Goshka's age.

'Well, this isn't much of a hole, chief!' said Gavrilov when they reached Goshka's trench. 'And it's not as if the ground's hard,' he added, pushing the spade in with his right leg, the healthy one.

'There wasn't much time,' Goshka took offence. 'But I'll finish it now. The moon's coming up.'

And true enough, the curl of the new moon had just climbed out of the black forest on the other bank, with clouds swirling round it like steam.

Goshka gave a whistle: 'There could easily be an air-raid tonight!' He reached out for the spade.

'Go and sleep,' said the captain angrily. 'You can finish this tomorrow.'

You were thinking exactly the same – you're just a boy yourself, he said to himself as he went down to the bridge. 'I don't want to see you here again till morning!' he shouted, turning round. Goshka trudged back, dejected.

The bridge was old and well-built: the railings were secure and the planks did not spring up when you walked on them. The second bridge, the railway bridge, could be seen about a mile to the left, just as the map indicated, and a road – paved rather than asphalted – entered the woods just in front of it. On Gavrilov's map the road and the railway line continued without crossing each other for about five kilometres until they both disappeared in a tear in the paper, and what happened to them thereafter was unclear – both on the map and in reality. Judging by the silence, the Germans could have been a hundred or a hundred and fifty kilometres away, but since the station was in ruins and the line had not been repaired (not to mention the fact that the chief engineer had not turned up), it was quite impossible to predict what might happen.

The absence of the engineers worried him less than the bombed-out station. Engineers are a slovenly lot, he thought, remembering the fortifications engineer in their regiment, a pimply, badly-shaven, good-for-nothing so-and-so, who constantly reeked of sweat and booze. They're supposed to be intelligent people, but they're just a bunch of layabouts . . . 'Course, maybe it's different when they're on civilian work, he admitted to himself, trying to be fair.

But the fact that the station had not been repaired, and that reserves and ammunition were not flooding through it – in short, that it was not needed – could not help but suggest to him that all was not well ahead. And the telephone conversation which had so cheered him two hours earlier now turned out to be not at all cheering.

What twaddle! Gavrilov suddenly felt enraged as he remembered, with perfect clarity, the voice on the line: 'They'll send goods-vans for you – goods-vans or engineers!' 'Crap!' He spat. He was now walking deeper into the woods on the other bank . . . He doesn't know – so he just opens his mouth and lets his belly rumble! I'd like to see him here, with his promises.

And to his sorrow he remembered that the man at the Moscow end of the line had not given his name.

And I didn't take the receipt . . . thought Gavrilov, dropping his head. What bad luck! Striding through the empty forest, he tried to fight off despair. Give me a platoon of soldiers, even a section, to command, instead of these women, he grumbled, forgetting his wounded lung and leg. 'Where are these women going to go if the Germans suddenly appear?' he said aloud and remembered that under his greatcoat he was wearing his old field-shirt – from his days as a political instructor – which clearly showed the places where the stars had been torn off. (His commander's field-shirt had been ripped open in the field hospital, where he had been carried over a comrade's shoulder, to try to stop the blood-flow from his lung.)

Serafima hoarded every last rag of clothing! – Gavrilov thought ill of his wife for the first time since their separation, but immediately pushed her to the back of his mind: Can a captain allow himself to be taken prisoner? Of course not; even the student mustn't. So what's the option: if you abandon the women you're a coward, if you don't you're a traitor to your country. What could be worse than having girls under your command?! He spat in annoyance. Well, wounded men – that would be worse, I suppose, he thought, and, picturing the church full of seriously injured soldiers instead of women, he cooled down a little.

'There's always someone who's worse off,' he said loudly, regaining his self-control. I've got two magazines and the student has cartridge pouches on his belt. That will have to do, he concluded, trying to force his thoughts away from this subject.

I mustn't panic, he thought. Perhaps the trenches *are* needed. If they sent us to dig them, they must be. And there has just been a mix-up with the engineers. I must stop thinking: seven bullets for the enemy, the eighth for me. They know what they're doing . . . His thoughts returned to his new Moscow bosses.

Two days before, in the briefing-room, where he had gone straight from hospital, his request to be sent to his regiment had been met with an abrupt response: 'This is also front-line work.'

At the time he had felt slighted, thinking that the civilian Tozhanov had intended the words 'front-line' in the loose sense – just as 'Stakhanovite' work-teams and important construction projects were sometimes called 'front-line'. But now Gavrilov tended to the idea that Tozhanov knew something Gavrilov did not, when he announced that Moscow was also 'the front'. This realization hurt Gavrilov, but at the same time eased his mind.

Looking at his watch, he saw that he had been walking for eighteen minutes, and the two kilometres he must have covered had added nothing to the silence. It was even quieter in the forest than at the church.

'I can't keep walking for ever,' sighed Gavrilov, and turned back. In any case, I'd better let the student get some sleep. He himself decided not to sleep until just before dawn, when the women would start digging and it would be a little warmer.

Goshka, offended by the captain, did not return to the church but waited until Gavrilov had crossed the bridge and then went down to the river. Here, catching his foot on a stone in the darkness, he fell and hurt himself, and cursed mildly as water seeped inside his left boot.

Something white splashed in the river and called out.

'Stop! Who's there?' shouted Goshka, before he had even time to be scared.

'Turn round, please,' said a plaintive voice, and Goshka guessed that it must be the redhead, Liya.

'Excuse me,' he mumbled.

Poor thing, he thought, fancy bathing in that water . . . I'll get her to work on my trench tomorrow. She can just scrape about a bit, and even up the parapet. Goshka felt like a caring commander.

He walked round the church. The driver was sitting smoking in the truck, with his long legs stuck out of the open cabin door.

'Can you give me a light?' asked Goshka cheerfully, not to save a match but in the hope of a conversation.

'You're too small – it will stunt your growth,' the student moralized, but gave him a light. He too was apprehensive – to say the least – left alone with three hundred women who were dead to the world. Without them he would not have been afraid. On his own, he would just have driven over the bridge and raced along the other bank – the wheel in his hands, his carbine hanging behind him in the cabin, and enough cartridges on his belt. He had been in the army for two years, but never at the front, and, never having seen it, did not fear death. But now, left alone with the sleeping women, he felt ill at ease, just like the captain across the river, scared by the uncertainty of what could happen if German tanks suddenly appeared. You could not protect the women, but nor could you desert them. And if they saw that the women were with you, an armed soldier, they might consider them to be mobilized, and deal with them accordingly . . .

'Sit down, since you're smoking,' said the student generously, moving over for Goshka. 'What street are you from?'

Like all relative newcomers to Moscow, the student loved to impress natives of the city with his knowledge of its streets. This helped ease his nostalgia for his own home town, and the Transport Institute, where he had spent only two months. His knowledge of Moscow allowed him to consider that he had been lucky none the less, because driving was more like work than military service, which he – like all city lads – was not exactly keen on in peacetime.

'Do you know Nogin Square?' Goshka replied.

'Yes. Near the Central Committee. They've surrendered Kharkov – that's my town. Have you heard?'

'Yes,' said Goshka with an understanding nod, then asked politely, after the requisite pause: 'Is your family still there?'

'Only cousins. My close family was evacuated. But it's still a shame – for the city. Have you been to Kharkov?'

'I'm afraid not,' Goshka answered modestly, having scarcely set foot outside of Moscow.

'It's a nice place.' Having kept silent for most of the day, the driver now said something in the darkness which he would never have dared to say in broad daylight: 'What about the Jerries, then – will you let them through?'

'Like hell I will!'

'Hmm. And how will you stop them?'

What is he, a defeatist? thought Goshka, not knowing whether to jump out or wait for the captain.

'It's always like that with us: big words, but no action. Besides . . . the situation is very serious,' the student added sadly.

'I understand that,' Goshka agreed.

'Of course you don't, said the driver, putting his arm round him, and Goshka again did not know whether to appreciate the soldier's warm gesture or to push him away as a coward and a panic-monger.

'You don't understand it at all, lad. And neither do I.' The driver suddenly changed his doleful tone: 'Well, how much have you dug?'

'Up to here.' Goshka knocked his knee with his hand.

'Don't dig too hard. Save your strength for tomorrow.'

'Are they bringing weapons?'

'Weapons! They're sending a train to take you all back to Moscow. Or more likely, they won't, and you'll have to walk back. So dig if you must, but don't overstrain yourself.'

'It's not true!' Goshka moved back. 'Do you know what you could get for saying things like that?'

'Huh, nonsense. Or do you regard me as a panic-monger? Go and report me.'

'I never said that . . . But we shan't surrender Moscow.'

'I'm not speaking about Moscow, I'm speaking about you.' The student spat. 'They brought you here, but where's the command? Where are the engineers? Is that football in the long coat supposed to be an engineer? The last time he dug a hole was under Potyomkin,* and that was probably for a latrine. Why do you

* Catherine II's favourite, General Grigory Potyomkin (1739–91) [Tr.]

59

think the captain and I drove fifteen miles at top speed today? To phone Moscow! Still, don't fret. I'll give you a hand tomorrow. Can't have you getting captured – you're not a woman.'

'What about you?'

'What about me? I've got a carbine, the captain's got his pistol. We'll be all right.' The driver spoke in such a straightforward manner that he won Goshka's confidence.

'But just you, er, keep all that to yourself, eh?' The driver suddenly sounded flustered. 'I told you that man to man. Right?'

'I won't breathe a word,' said Goshka, and thought: he's not so bad. Just nervous. But the situation really is grave.

'Are you asleep, student?' came Gavrilov's voice. 'You better go and kip down now.'

'How are things, Comrade Captain?' asked the driver brightly.

'Get moving,' he hissed at Goshka.

'Quiet. Absolutely normal. Why aren't you sleeping?' Gavrilov snapped at the young volunteer. Like all commanders, he could not bear to see soldiers hanging about doing nothing. 'Do you think this is a young pioneers' camp?'

'The likes of him would get hell in a pioneer camp!' said the student derisively, immediately dissociating himself from the young lad to whom only a minute before he had been revealing his nocturnal fears. 'When are you going to sleep, Comrade Captain?'

'In the morning. You have nicer dreams in the morning.'

9

Liya had sat under the bridge plucking up the courage to strip and go into the water. Like most of the women she had only quickly washed her hands and face before supper, intending to forgo her usual thorough evening ablutions. 'It's not good to stand out,' she tried to excuse herself. But a voice was arguing with her: 'You'll go to ruin, my girl.' It was the sad voice of Yelena Fedotovna, the tall lady from the flat opposite. 'No, I mustn't stand out,' Liya repeated before supper, and this time Yelena Fedotovna said nothing.

But now, on the empty riverbank, bending invisibly over Liya, she whispered in a sharp, bitter voice (just as before, in the lift): 'We have no one else to rely on now.'

And Liya took off her coat and began to unlace her mother's hateful boots.

That day in the lift – it was at the time when her father was in trouble – Liya had flu, and was all wrapped up in scarves, coughing and blowing her nose. Failing to turn away quickly enough, she had sneezed over the tall, rather ungainly woman who had recently moved into their block.

'Oh, I'm sorry, excuse me!' Liya turned to face the wall, still sneezing.

'It's all right, my girl,' replied the woman. 'I know you,' she added, meaningfully. 'You ought to wash in icy water. Icy water and physical exercise. We have no one else to rely on now,' the strange woman said and got out of the lift first.

Later, when Liya mulled over these words, they often seemed insulting to her, for her father was at least with her, whereas this lanky woman's husband was goodness knows where, but at the time Liya had felt so drawn to Yelena Fedotovna that she remained standing on the landing for a long time, staring at her door as though some fairy prince or opera star had vanished through it. '*We*', she had said, and into this word Liya read sadness and affection, stubborn pride and the respect of a grown woman for a sixteen-year-old girl, and even, perhaps, the promise of unselfish and unspoken friendship. Meeting her afterwards, Liya always blushed with joy and Yelena Fedotovna smiled at her amiably, and that was more meaningful than words. In any case, what could they say to each other when, via the chatterbox Ganya, Yelena Fedotovna already knew all about Liya's family, and Liya also knew this and that about the unhappy woman but did not wish to intrude or reopen an unhealed wound. At first Liya would also smile to Yelene Fedotovna's bespectacled daughter, Karina, but she used to reply once with a sort of haughty nod of the head, and once, in the lift, thinking Liya could not see her in the mirror, she stuck out her tongue. But Liya scarcely minded, realizing that Karina was just a child and that, for all Yelena Fedotovna's efforts, her childhood was not at all easy.

'Brrrr!' shuddered Liya as she stepped into the icy water, requiring a desperate effort not to jump straight out again. It felt as if sharp pieces of ice were cutting off her feet. 'I must,' she sighed, wading in up to her knees and pulling off her sweater and skirt over her head.

Her back and shoulders felt less cold than her legs, and looking at her shoulder-blades and small breasts with undisguised malice, she began rubbing them ruthlessly with the freezing water.

'It really has made a big difference, she had shyly admitted to Yelena Fedotovna a year before, when they had bumped into each other again in the lift.

'Yes. Congratulations,' she nodded, forgetting about the icy water and assuming that Liya was speaking about her father's rehabilitation. 'You'll be able to study again now.'

'I don't know . . . Mother is very unwell . . .'

'I'm sorry,' her neighbour said abruptly, and Liya understood that she considered Liya's father to be a heartless man.

Of course, thought Liya, she feels sorry for my mother – such a good woman, and a husband like that . . . But maybe he is not such a rotter, merely weak-willed, and people take advantage of his lack of character. Men are often like that . . .

Suddenly she let out a shriek, seeing Goshka slipping at the side of the river. Goshka coyly walked away.

Tactful, thought Liya, her mind wandering from Goshka to the handsome Viktor, whom Sanka had met in the summer in the Park of Culture.

She rubbed her thin body roughly with a towel. 'No, it wasn't Rio de Janeiro!' she repeated to herself bitterly.

And now she relived that last Monday before the war . . . In the evening the telephone had rung.

'It'll be for me!' said Sanka, bustling out of the room. Then her surprised voice could be heard in the corridor: 'Liya? Who's speaking?' Her soprano seemed to leap to the ceiling, turn a triple salto, and dive like a hawk into the receiver. 'But it's me, Alexandra. Didn't you recognize me?' Sanka gushed in the corridor, having no intention of calling Liya. 'Wait at Dzerzhinsky Square. I'll be there in two minutes,' she said and immediately came flying into the room.

'I'll go and get my man some things,' she said, rummaging in Liya's purse for a five-rouble note. 'D'you think he'll drink fortified wine? You tidy up a bit while I'm gone!' And, grabbing Liya's bag (the same one as they had with them now, containing bread, their documents and towels) she dashed out of the flat.

Forty minutes later Viktor rang three times and Liya, afraid of bumping into Sanka's mother or Ganya (who spent more time lounging about their flat than Yelena Fedotovna's), opened the door.

'Excuse me for coming empty-handed,' said the student, spreading his arms. 'I wasn't intending to come visiting.'

Liya stood before him, indecisive and small, and her shyness transmitted itself to him.

'This way,' she finally uttered, and led the student into their room, but did not close the door completely. 'Sanka will be back in a minute.'

She said this purely for the sake of saying something, and blushed at once. It sounded as if she herself understood, and agreed in advance, that the young man had come not to see them both, but only Sanka.

'Yes, she told me,' the student nodded, also blushing. He himself was no longer sure whom he had come to see, and felt awkward.

Sanka flew in – noisy and bustling, and without a trace of gaucherie.

'Kettle on? I'll do it, just a sec,' she chirped, as though she had been entertaining young men all her life, rather than indulging in it for the first time.

'I'm not actually hungry,' said Viktor in embarrassment.

'What's hunger got to do with it?!' Sanka noisily emptied the contents of her bag on to the table: a bottle of fortified wine, a tin of sprats, and two hundred grammes each of sausage and cheese.

Liya obediently went to boil the kettle. She was met in the kitchen by Ganya, who, in view of the interesting guest, was in no hurry to get back to her cottage on the Iksha: 'Just look at that! She's only just buried her mother . . .'

'Call Alexandra,' barked Sanka's mother.

'Your mother wants you,' said Liya, returning to the room.

'Oops, I'm for it!' Sanka giggled. 'Don't get bored here, I'll be back in half a mo!'

'Noisy character, isn't she!' Viktor smiled.

'She's nice,' Liya corrected him, trying to be neither angry nor envious of her friend.

'Do you live together?'

'No. I mean – yes. That is, Sanka lives with me. For the time being . . . She looked after my mother a lot . . .' Liya explained, and, blushing again, added: 'My mother's dead,' lest the young man should think that Sanka was some kind of domestic.

He nodded. He had a nice face – not just handsome but also very intelligent. Liya would have liked just to sit with him and chat, but she did not know how to begin a conversation, and was afraid of appearing forward. Realizing that her friend was about to rush in, she repeated the same silliness as before: 'Sanka will be back in a second.'

'Oh, parents, really!' exclaimed Sanka, bursting into the room. 'What have you been doing? The bread's not cut, the tin's not opened. Honestly, Liya! Don't be so shy, he won't eat you. He's a Muscovite, same as us!'

'I'm from Saratov,' said the student.

'Really? You can't tell from your accent. Still, since you're in Moscow we'll call you a Muscovite! Here, open this. That's a man's job!' She held out the tin-opener for him.

Liya clinked glasses with them three times but only sipped at her wine, and kept making as if to leave.

'Wait until Mum goes to bed, and then . . .' Sanka would whisper to her each time. Finally the radio broadcast its final news bulletin, the Kremlin clock struck midnight, and Liya took a thick notebook and a physics manual from her bookshelf and quietly went through to the kitchen. Ganya, thank God, had left, and the flat was asleep. Liya shut the door softly, lit the meagre kitchen light, and sat at the table. 'The right-hand rule . . . rod and coil . . .' She tried to concentrate, but the laws of magnetic induction just would not sink in, because her thoughts kept running away from the textbook and tiptoeing back to the room, where something great and secret was about to take place.

If the right hand is pointed along the rod, then the four fingers will show the direction of electric current in the coil winding . . . 'I don't understand a thing.' She tried to drown her thoughts in physics. 'What if she has a baby? It would be a very beautiful one,' she said out loud, and just at that moment Sanka's mother opened the door and started telling Liya off for using up 'common electricity'.

'Go to bed, you sponger!'

'No, I won't,' said Liya firmly.

'Oh won't you now! I'll just have to drag you there. Think you should get your own way?!' And she hauled Liya into the corridor.

'Oh, it's locked. Sanka, what have you locked the door for? Open up!' She hammered on the door.

An unimaginable scandal ensued. The neighbours immediately appeared at their doors. Sanka's drunken father, the house-manager, stood gaping senselessly as Sanka fended off her mother and let the frightened student through to the front door.

'You've ruined the girl!' cried her mother, at the same time beating the girl with her fists.

'Ssh, Mother,' whispered Sanka. 'Think of the neighbours!'

'It's bedtime,' grumbled the neighbours, but for some reason they did not go to their beds.

'And you're a fine one!' Sanka suddenly let fly at Liya. 'Hanging around in the kitchen all night! The months I spent looking after that old witch of yours, you could have gone to the station for one night. You're a bitch, that's what you are!' And, snatching her bed-linen and dresses from the wardrobe, she stormed out of Liya's room.

Liya sobbed until dawn, realizing that Sanka was right, but she could not make the first move towards reconciliation, after Sanka had called her mother an old witch. Two days later the house-manager, who was aware that Liya was now living alone in her room, caused another ugly scene. He threatened to take away her room, and then started to harass her in his drunkenness, until Sanka appeared and dealt him an almighty blow on the back and another on the neck. The girls made up and forgave each other. They sobbed and embraced, and, exhausted, Liya finally asked: 'Aren't you afraid you'll have a baby?'

Sanka gave a wave of her hand, jokingly, as if to say, in the words of the proverb: 'If you're afraid of wolves, you don't go into the forest.' And her smile was both sly and proud, although the student (Liya was almost certain about this) never rang Sanka again.

10

'Yes, life's a struggle!' sighed Liya, climbing the hill. Her father often used to repeat that phrase, usually quite out of place. And having said it now, also out of place, Liya smiled to herself and went into the church. Everyone was asleep apart from Goshka, who was sitting on a stool beside a joiner's bench.

'Sit down,' he said, straightening himself before Liya, who had just come out of the freezing water.

He's such a nice boy; I hope that selfish girl Karina doesn't spoil him, thought Liya, forgetting that Goshka was here, at the trenches, whereas Karina and her mother were now far from Moscow. Only yesterday – no, the day before, in the morning – Liya had overcome her shyness and gone to say goodbye to the Ryzhovs.

'You're leaving, and so am I,' she had said. 'I've signed up for the trenches.'

'How I envy you, my girl,' said Yelena Fedotovna, getting up from the floor, where she was vainly trying to tie up a suitcase with two scarves.

'What Mum means is that I am getting in the way of her heroism,' said Karina caustically.

'What do you mean, Karina?' said her huge mother, taken aback. 'I am very fond of you and respect you,' she turned again to Liya. 'Do take care of yourself.'

'I wanted to go to the front, but they wouldn't take me. Perhaps from the trenches I'll be able to . . .'

'Yes, I understand you, my girl. But look after yourself, please. Let me at least cross you.'

'Mum!' shouted Karina.

'I'm an atheist,' said Liya softly, feeling awkward.

'I know. So am I. But who else can we rely on now?' She crossed Liya clumsily. 'Don't worry,' she whispered, 'Christ is for everyone. But stay alive, my dear . . .'

'Aren't you cold?' asked Goshka, studying the red-haired girl with curiosity.

'Not at all! It's invigorating. Yelena Fedotovna recommended me to do it,' she said, as though apologizing for going into the cold October stream on her own. 'Karina will be on her way by now, I suppose,' she hurried to change the subject.

'Probably,' Goshka agreed. 'Aren't you going to sleep?'

'I don't know. I don't think I'll be able to.'

Poor girl, he thought, and said: 'I can't sleep either.'

'That's because there are so many impressions all at once,' said Liya. 'Do you think we'll get a lot of digging done tomorrow?'

'We'll see. The situation is very serious.'

'I can imagine.'

'Can you keep a military secret?' Goshka suddenly blurted out, bursting with what he had heard from the driver.

'I don't know. I've never been told one.'

'But can you give your word?' he exclaimed with vexation, afraid that any minute now he would divulge military secrets to her without having received any assurances.

'Yes,' Liya smiled, 'I can give you "Komsomol's honour". Will that do?'

'Right,' he said joyfully. 'The situation is very complex. We may have to leave here.'

'How?' whispered Liya, puzzled.

'Probably on foot,' he interrupted her question. 'They promised a train, but that's unlikely.'

'I'm sorry, but that can't be true. Don't be angry, but I don't believe you. How do you know?'

'I know.'

'Did the captain tell you?'

'It doesn't matter. Only, don't think I'm a coward.'

'Don't be silly, I'm not thinking anything. But I just can't believe it. And why did he tell only you? Why not everybody? I don't get it. Goshka, tell me, are you joking?'

They were speaking in whispers in a huge church, full of snoring, but it seemed to Liya as if Goshka was shouting at her through a megaphone.

'I wanted to go to the front,' Liya whispered quickly, 'but they didn't take me. They would only allow me to work in a hospital, as a nurse. But I was a nurse already – at home . . .' She dropped her eyes, as though afraid of offending her dead mother. 'I know how to use a rifle,' she said hopefully again, as though Goshka was the chief armourer.

'If they'd given me a rifle I wouldn't have come here,' said Goshka.

'Nor I,' sighed Liya.

Goshka looked at her doubtfully but said nothing. He did not wish to spoil such a good night-time conversation. In the abandoned church, among the sleeping women, only the two of them were keeping vigil. Two paraffin-lamps were burning. Through a broken window he could see the edge of a cloud lit by the moon. The night was quiet, perhaps the first sleepless night in his whole life, apart from a few nights on the roof during air-raids. But then the roofs and garrets had been full of people: here it was just the two of them.

She's not bad, he thought . . . 'Courageous' – that was the word. She bathed in freezing water. Brrr! He imagined the cold. Shooting isn't the same as digging: maybe she really can do it . . . He felt well disposed towards her, either because of her loneliness or because she had spoken to him as an adult and had not sent him off to sleep.

'The situation is very complicated,' he said once more, investing the words with much less significance than they had for Liya. Despite the fact that the Germans were marching over his country, and although, from his decent knowledge of geography, combined with the Information Office reports (albeit a week or a week and a half late) he knew where the front line now was, the general situation did not alarm him much. Indeed he considered the war no less than a tremendous stroke of luck for him personally, and now, when he was almost at the front, he was impatient to get even closer to it, to receive a rifle, a hand machine-gun or a Maxim (a Shpagin was beyond his wildest dreams) and to do what real men do in films. He was a bright lad and could supply sensible answers to many questions, but for the moment his whole being was still stupider than his brain, and he was straining forward, to that place beyond the river and the silence, where he imagined the whole world was shooting, banging, exploding, burning, flaring up, and shouting 'hurrah!'

Although older than Goshka, Liya felt so close to him now, almost like a sister, that she suddenly asked him, startling herself with her own boldness: 'How did all this happen anyway? Did we believe Hitler?'

'It was diplomatic cunning!' he said dismissively, still feeling elated by the machine-gun fire and the sight of Germans falling, with their rifles up in the air.

'No, don't say that . . . I really don't understand.' Once emboldened, Liya would not give up. 'I want to help. Or not even help, but do *something*. Even if it's just digging trenches . . . But you say . . .'

'Don't worry, we'll beat the Germans.'

'Yes, I know . . . but, you can't just sit and do nothing. You know,' she lowered her whisper, 'my father got into difficulties. But I didn't just console him. I forced him to write letters, and complaints, and requests, and explanations, to every conceivable official. I didn't let him sit idly. I kept pestering him to act. If you do nothing, you can go mad . . . you can go to the dogs . . . you can even stop washing . . .'

'Yes, of course,' Goshka nodded, not entirely sure.

'You know, I keep thinking: there are far more of us – we've got two or three times as many people as the Nazis. If every one of us killed one Nazi, and died himself – we would still win! I am ready to die myself, but first I want to kill one Hitlerite.'

'They ride in armoured cars. Bullets won't reach them.'

'So what do we do? And where are our armoured cars? We've got them too – remember, before the parades the tanks used to wake us at night.'

'That's right! You and I are from the same block!' Goshka sounded overjoyed for some reason. 'Aren't we?'

'Yes!' Liya smiled, not seeing what was so surprising about it: Sanka was from the same block too, and so were many of the other women.

'Do you like singing?' he asked, as if this was the crux of the matter.

'Yes, but only to myself. My voice is terrible.'

'So is mine. I only sing in my mind. Let me sing my favourite song to you, and you guess what it is from my eyes.'

'I can't,' smiled Liya, feeling flattered. 'I'm useless at that kind of thing.'

'No, no, you'll manage it! Look!' He compressed his lips, inflated his nostrils, and kept his eyes quite still. He was barely breathing.

'Well?' he asked at last, his face as red as if he had been carrying a hundredweight sack.

69

'I don't know, I'm afraid of being wrong,' said Liya. 'At the end I felt as if it went: "where the horses trample on the bodies . . ."'

'That's right!' he exclaimed with delight. ' "Useless at that kind of thing"! You're a clairvoyant!'

Fighting his tiredness, Gavrilov strolled around the church, went down to the river and splashed his face, then climbed the hill and walked round the church again. The driver was too big for his cabin and was sleeping with his long legs stuck outside. His boots were somewhat newer than Gavrilov's. The wind came in gusts, and the roofing iron on the church whined a sad song, rather like 'The Hills of Manchuria', Gavrilov fancied – but then, he sang all songs to the same tune, choosing the words according to his mood.

'It's all working for the Germans!' he thought about everything at once – the wind, the weather, and the situation in which he and his country had landed, against their will. And suddenly, looking upwards for the umpteenth time with a feeling of anger and bitterness, he spotted an aircraft wing slipping over a corner of the moon, and then, through the wind, he discerned the drone of bombers. There was evidently a fair number of them: a minute later another crossed the blade of the moon. They were flying high – too high for him to recognize them – but they were flying directly above the main highway and he realized that they were heading for Moscow. Since the outbreak of the war he had seen so few Soviet planes that he assumed every flying object to be alien until he could make out the markings clearly. It was easier that way: better safe than sorry. And the rare exceptions, when the Soviet star would flash into view as the plane came into land or entered sunlight, were like a bonus.

'It's him they're after . . . And we are all defending him,' said Gavrilov sorrowfully, remembering the abandoned towns, especially Slutsk, where Simka and his children remained. 'They are protecting him, they won't surrender,' he repeated, hearing as though in a dream the distant shots of the anti-aircraft batteries, like soft, rapid heartbeats.

'He has a clearer view from up there,' Gavrilov had always believed, until that daybreak when the alarm was sounded and they were woken and moved out to meet the advancing enemy tank formations, without even the chance to go to Slutsk to bid their wives farewell.

And for ten days, seeing Germans ahead and above him, Gavrilov waited for a word from the man who knew everything and saw everything, but Stalin was silent. Only when they were across the Dnieper did they receive his speech, which took up both sides of the divisional news-sheet, and all around heaved a sigh, but Gavrilov sank into thought.

The speech worried him, because of one phrase: 'there are no invincible armies.' After all, nothing Stalin said was ever simple and straightforward. Even six years earlier, when he had made his arrogant claim that 'life has become better, life has become happier, Comrades', even those words could not be taken literally but had to be applied to the future – meaning that a time would come when things really would be a bit better and happier.

And, having grown accustomed to taking every word from above as a programme for the future, Gavrilov read the phrase about invincible armies – intended to raise spirits and inspire confidence in victory – as a hint that anything could happen.

It was late in the evening. He came out of his hut, called the commander of the first company, and gave the order to dig in.

'The men are tired . . . And the place is so exposed . . .' the senior lieutenant tried to dissuade Gavrilov.

'Do you want a bullet through your head?' asked the captain in a gravelike whisper, and the lieutenant – alone, and not recognizing his battalion commander – suddenly saw himself, his country, and the situation at the front in a different light.

The place was indeed flat and bare. The tanks overran them in the first half-hour, and Gavrilov immediately forget that he was no longer a political instructor, but a battalion commander, and jumped up on to a parapet with a pistol and shouted the battle-cry they had used at manoeuvres: 'For the Motherland, for Stalin!' A burst of German tank-fire pierced his lung, and his leg twice.

As he recalled that July morning, he looked up at the sky again. The aeroplanes were gone, but even without them he felt empty and cold. He went into the church to see if there was any warm porridge left in a bucket. Beside the work-bench, a girl in a coat was sitting with her back to the captain, and opposite her, leaning againgst the bench, stood the lad who had earlier shown the captain his trench. The boy was looking at the girl and did not see the captain. At first Gavrilov thought they were playing at outstaring each other, because the boy's face was so tensed up it looked as if it was about to burst. But then the girl said something about horses and dead bodies, and the captain, concluding that it was not love but sheer mischief, sent them off to sleep.

11

In the morning the women carried the buckets out of the church, scraped out the previous day's porridge, and set about making more. The old man, Mikhail Fyodorich, arrived from the village freshly shaven ('like a baby' thought the captain, feeling his own two-days' growth).

'What are your directions? Did you get through to Moscow?' He stood to attention before the captain and all but saluted him.

'There's only one direction: to dig. Aeroplanes flew over twice during the night.' Gavrilov lowered his voice. 'We've got to dig, Granddad.'

The captain's voice somehow jarred with the old man's mood. He reminded Gavrilov about the anti-tank barriers.

'My helpers did some cutting yesterday; now they'll start welding. Where do you want the first ones positioned?'

'We'll decide that later – they won't run away,' said Gavrilov shortly. 'What we should really be using are girders, of course, not rails . . . Oh, never mind. It'll all work out, Granddad,' he said, to end the conversation somehow. 'Excuse me. I haven't slept for two nights.'

The student, who stood in for the captain, treated himself to baked potatoes, supped boiling porridge straight from a pail, and then hung around feeling bored until the next mealtime. He had already walked all round the future defensive positions three times, keeping his distance from the perky girls, who never missed an opportunity to take a rest from digging and tease him: 'Hey, give's a hand!', 'Come here and warm me up!', 'Don't be lonely, lad!' – things like that. If there had been only two or three of them he would have been able to joke back, but such a huge bunch of them intimidated him. So instead he walked about with a serious, gloomy face, beside the little Mikhail Fyodorich, who had been beaming like a bridegroom ever since morning.

'We'll join up the trenches later, for good communications. And tomorrow we can make a dug-out. The railway sleepers aren't serving any purpose now – we'll use them as flooring.'

'The sleepers are too short,' said the student curtly. The fussy old man was annoying him intensely.

'Have you seen the anti-tank barriers?' boasted the old man a minute later. 'Come and look!' And he led the driver over the road, to where two-metre lengths of rail, welded together in crosses, were lying in the ditch.

'We've used three lengths per barrier. Do you think that is enough? Four would be rather too heavy for the boys to move,' he said in justification.

'It should do,' the student yawned.

'Girders, of course, would be better against tanks. But where can we get hold of them? We have to make do with what comes to hand.'

'Uh-huh,' nodded the student.

'I have already reported to the comrade captain,' Mikhail Fyodorich prattled on, 'that I consider it essential to blow up the railway bridge. The station is out of action anyway, and no trains are moving westwards. With the bridge there, the Germans could take us on the flank.'

'Who, the women?!' said the student sarcastically.

'Oh, sorry. I mean the Red Army men who will take our positions.' Mikhail Fyodorich did not want to lose a drop of enthusiasm.

'They'll blow it up themselves,' replied the student, having not the slightest desire to think about anybody occupying these trenches, far less blowing up the railway bridges on their left flank. 'I wonder if I should wake the captain – he might want to eat,' he thought, though perfectly well aware that a man who has not slept for two nights does not wish to be woken even for food.

The old man was still going on: 'I understand you, Comrade soldier. There are a great many of them and they are ill-disciplined.' He nodded towards the women. 'Of course, *they* might discipline them.' He pointed to the woods, high above which three groups of planes were flying.

'They're not for them,' the student grimaced.

'Are they ours?' said the old man with delight, but the student did not reply. His sharp young eyes had immediately recognized

73

the aeroplanes as Junkers-87s – the same as those which had flown in the same direction two hours earlier, when he was helping himself to porridge. They had flown very high, and had evidently returned at the same height because he had not noticed them (and, try as he might, he could not believe they had all been shot down). These ones were flying lower, so that even the bespectacled old man could see them, but he could not make out the crosses on their wings, thank goodness. The women, too, paid them scant attention: only two or three of them craned their necks for a moment and shielded their eyes against the weak sun, and then went on digging again.

'What a day, eh?' sighed the old man. 'A real Indian summer, if a little late.'

'A German summer, you mean.'

'Don't you worry, Comrade soldier,' the old man reassured him. 'After such a sudden warm spell there will be hail – or even a real snowstorm. The Germans will freeze.'

'I don't suppose the women will be exactly warm, either,' replied the student and walked away towards the church.

I wonder if he's awake yet, he hoped, but the captain was still asleep, with the cabin doors tightly shut. One of the filthy windows was rolled down just a fraction, and the student could see how awkwardly the captain was sleeping: his belt was not unbuckled, but merely slackened off a little, and his eyes were covered with his peak-cap.

The student went back to the fire and drank some tea with the cooks. They were nearly all middle-aged – old enough to be his mother – and he was less shy with them. Some of them had sons at the front.

'There's been no word from mine for over two weeks,' one of them sighed.

'Nor mine . . .'

'Mine hasn't written either.'

'You haven't met him, have you?' they all asked the driver, giving their sons' names, and when he explained that he had not been at the front yet, since he was attached to the Moscow defences, they seemed not to be envious, but genuinely pleased for him, for not being right in the firing line.

'Have some more tea, son!'

'He'd drink more if it was vodka!'

'No, he's not a drinker – his face is pure.'

'Thank you,' he said, and after the third mugful, feeling confident enough to ignore the giggling trench-diggers, he set off down the hill to see the young Goshka.

He actually felt like going farther, to the railway bridge, where some young girls who looked like students were digging. He had noticed them long ago because they tended to stick together, either because they were from the same institute, or perhaps because they simply enjoyed each other's jolly company. Either way, they were a cheerful bunch, and paid no attention to the driver. He would have liked to have gone up to them, but was too shy and stopped beside Goshka.

He was already up to his neck in his little trench, and above him, on the breastwork, a red-haired girl in a short coat and high tan boots, with blue ski-pants showing under her skirt, was pottering about.

'Not bad, eh?' Goshka cried from the depths, and the eternally sceptical student nodded his head in agreement so as not to offend the girl. She may have been ugly, with her rye-coloured eyelashes and huge freckles, but she had such an air of oppression or confusion about her that to speak cruelly to her amounted to disrespecting oneself.

'What are you staring at?' Sanka cried behind him. 'We're hard at it too, you know!'

'They're calling you,' said Liya nervously.

'They can wait . . . Let me show you how,' he said, taking her spade. 'And don't be embarrassed, put on your gloves,' he added in a quieter voice, as though he had instantly guessed Liya's true nature. Liya blushed and looked with hatred at the palms of her little hands with their huge white blisters.

'Hey, driver, I'm no good, neither. Come and teach me!' Sanka shouted from her trench.

'How come they all go for these ginger-heads?' complained Ganya, nearby. 'My Klanka had a touch of ginger too.'

I've landed in it now, thought the student, his face turning crimson as he evened up the parapet. And I can't go away now – it would be a shame for the girl. They'll tease her to death.

'I understand, I understand. I'll do it now,' said Liya apologetically.

'It's all right,' said the student in a deep voice. 'There will be plenty of time for you to dig.'

'You mean we're staying here?' Goshka chipped in, raising his hand.

'Ssshh!' the student showed a clenched fist behind his back.

'OK. Mum's the word,' Goshka babbled, and flashed Liya a savage look. But the student intercepted the glance and realized that the greenhorn had been blabbing.

The girl also raised her head and smiled at the student as if to say: it's all right, the secret's safe with me. And the student, as though admitting his own indiscretion and reproaching himself for it, patted Liya on the shoulder – not just any old how, but as a friend, and she understood.

Hm, it's best to keep your mouth shut here, he reflected, surveying the hillside and the riverbank with annoyance. From bridge to bridge and a little beyond the highway, work was in full swing. The women were sinking as though into quicksand, and some of them were already lost up to their necks and shoulders.

'This trench is ready,' said the student. 'Let's start another.'

'Right-oh!' Liya nodded.

She looked wistfully at the young man, scarcely hoping to believe that she might have caught his fancy ... It's just that he has to dig *somewhere*. So he's lending a hand. And I happen to be the most incompetent, she said to herself, thinking about her hot blistered hands which were aching under her rough gloves. But he's very nice. Understanding. Probably has quite delicate feelings. There's even a touch of Viktor about him. Only Viktor ... Without completing her thought, she suddenly remembered something that her friend, who was swinging a pick over in her trench, did not know.

On the sixth day of the war, when Sanka and her mother went to see off her father, who had been mobilized, the telephone again rang in the corridor.

'Liya, this is the ill-fated Viktor.'

'Sanka isn't at home,' she replied drily.

'Liya, it's you I need ... Do you know the club at the woolmill? You'll have to take a "B" tram. Come on your own, though.'

'All right,' said Liya, understanding that he had been called up.

And when the following day, strangely transformed in an ill-fitting field-shirt, breeches, boots and puttees, he held her hands and gazed into her face, and whispered that she had impressed him right from the start and that he felt shy with her, whereas Sanka was so forward and pushy, and so on and so forth, Liya listened to him without taking her eyes off him, listened and did not believe him. And when, just before leaving, he began to kiss her, she did not turn her head away, but still she did not believe him. All men were weak, and this one was no exception, though he was an honest fellow. He felt guilty towards her and towards Sanka, wanted to justify himself, and therefore, despite his honesty, lied even more. No, he didn't need her. It was just out of superstition that he wanted someone to see him off on his way to the bombs, bullets, shells, and death . . . But he could not call Sanka – he felt too ashamed in front of her.

'I shall write to you,' said Viktor.

'Good,' she nodded, hoping that this sad farewell would soon be forgotten and that he would not write. For if Sanka found a letter in their box, the most awful misunderstandings could start up again – all the more so as Sanka's father, whom Liya had forgiven after he received his call-up papers, was at the front, whereas Liya's father, though he worked hard at his important militarized factory, was not in constant danger of losing his life.

And now, looking at the driver, she was more grieved than gratified by his care and attentiveness.

'Oh-ho! Carry on here without me,' he shouted, and jumping out of the shallow, newly started trench, he ran down the slope to the bridge.

'Where have you come from?' he called as he ran.

Liya saw that two soldiers in absolutely filthy greatcoats had appeared out of the woods on the other bank and were running towards the driver. 'What if they're Germans in disguise?' she thought with fright, seeing their filthy forage-caps, which were turned inside out and pulled down over their ears. But one of them was already embracing the driver. Then the other did the same, and the three of them leaned against the railing of the bridge cheerfully hugging each other's shoulders. The driver, even in his old field-shirt with its sweaty armpits, looked a real dandy beside the exhausted, dirty, unshaven soldiers. But it was clear that they were terribly glad to see him. Then the soldiers ran back into the woods, and the driver raced back to Liya and Goshka via the bridge, grabbed his coat, and, buttoning it on the move and ignoring Goshka's silent stare, he ran up to the church, presumably to wake the captain.

12

Only half-awake, Gavrilov imagined the very worst had happened. Somebody's face, full of anger, was hanging over him. Moreover, the face was twisted round so that the little star on the fur hat was lower than the shirt collar which was sticking out above a white sheepskin coat.

'Where did I go wrong?' The words echoed in his half-sleeping brain.

He raised his head, picked up his cap which had fallen on to the floor of the cabin, and unhurriedly got out. Before him stood a dashing lieutenant in a new sheepskin coat, holding a new machine-gun against his white chest. The points of his shirt collar had disappeared under his sheepskin again, but even before he got up Gavrilov had spotted that there were two bars on each.

'Were you sleeping?' asked the lieutenant in a slow, even tone.

'Is it forbidden?' Gavrilov snarled back. Now he could see that the lieutenant was alone: an Izh-8 motorcycle with no sidecar was propped up against the church behind him.

This one certainly likes his comforts! thought the captain, envying everything at once: his sheepskin coat, his fur hat with its ear-flaps, his new Shpagin machine-gun, and above all his motorcycle. All you need now is a feather bed, mate! he thought with a wry smile. About five yards away stood Maria Ivanovna.

She's sniffed him out, thought Gavrilov.

'Well?' he said.

'What d'you mean: "well"?' shouted the motorcyclist. 'Where are the Germans?'

'You tell me!' said Gavrilov, yawning intentionally, now fully aware that it was not him the lieutenant had come to see. He turned to Maria Ivanovna: 'Why did you let him wake me up for no reason?'

'What's it got to do with me?' she rejoined.

'Where's the enemy, captain?' the lieutenant repeated slowly.

'I'm "comrade captain" to you. Right?' said Gavrilov, turning pale as he caught a glimpse, as in a gun-sight, of a disdainful smirk on the woman commander's face. 'And stand to attention, will you!'

'OK, cool it,' said the motorcyclist, trying to deflate him.

'Where have you come from?'

'None of your business. I'm not your subordinate.'

'If you're not my subordinate, get on your tin bike and bugger off!' said Gavrilov, considering the conversation closed since the motorcyclist had lowered the tone. He had no particular desire to have anything to do with this fop in his sheepskin coat.

'Have you been here long?' asked the lieutenant in a much more normal tone.

'We arrived yesterday, ' Maria Ivanovna answered for Gavrilov.

'And nothing's happened?'

'Nothing, Comrade Commander.'

'Neither Germans nor our lads been here?'

'No.'

'Well, there's a thing!' said the smart lieutenant with a sigh.

'Drive on! You'll find out over there!' Gavrilov grinned, letting the lieutenant know that he had sensed both his confusion and his reluctance to cross the bridge. Gavrilov was now convinced that the lieutenant had been sent to assess the situation, and he would have liked to ask him whom he had been sent by, and how well off his superiors were for men and equipment, and whether they would send them here, to the trenches (or, better still, even farther, over the river), but he realised that this lieutenant in the smart new sheepskin coat would give absolutely nothing away, so instead Gavrilov merely repeated, mockingly: 'Drive on, and you'll find out all about it!'

'Have something hot to eat!' said Maria Ivanovna in a voice full of motherly care, and she went over to the camp fire.

'I suppose so,' murmured the lieutenant. He was now shuffling from foot to foot in front of the church, having lost more than half of his former swagger.

'Are you hungry?' asked Gavrilov, glancing at him again, but at that moment his attention was caught by the driver, running up from the trenches.

'Comrade Captain! Comrade Captain!' he panted. 'Some of our men are there.'

'Where?' exclaimed Gavrilov and the motorcyclist in unison.

'Just over the river. Some of them are wounded . . . they're bringing them now . . .'

Gavrilov and the lieutenant raced towards the bridge and

spotted the soldiers on the other side, looking more like tramps. Their coats were black and reddish, as though they had been crawling through a bog and rubbing themselves against tree-trunks or fallen leaves. Not one of them was wearing puttees, and their forage-caps were all turned inside out and pulled over their ears. First two soldiers appeared, carrying a third on what could have been a tarpaulin, a piece of tent, or a gun-case. The wounded man's right leg was also wound in tarpaulin of a darker colour, evidently soaked in blood. With a shriek the women threw down their spades and dashed to the bridge, overtaking the commanders.

'Let's wait,' said the lieutenant sternly. The captain did not reply. 'Let him command if he wants to,' he decided. 'Why should I butt in – I've enough to do with the women, and now there's these wounded, to boot.' Three more soldiers emerged from the woods, also looking like wood-demons. Two of them looked slightly injured: one had his arm bandaged, the other's arm hung limply at his side. The third hopped along on one leg, with his arms around their shoulders; his other leg was wrapped in a torn-off coat sleeve and tied round with telephone wire. Behind them two more Red Army men carried a badly wounded comrade on a makeshift stretcher. The women embraced the soldiers on the bridge and helped to carry the wounded man, weeping and wailing.

'Perhaps you should buzz over to the hospital,' Gavrilov said quietly to the student.

'But they've promised a train . . .' replied the driver, also quietly, implying that he was not inclined to leave the captain alone here with all these women.

'It could take three years for that promise to . . .' Gavrilov sighed. 'All right, we'll wait a while. Heat up the engine meanwhile and check everything's in order.'

'Oh, Lord, so young . . .'

'Good grief!'

'The monsters, how can they do this to people?!' the women cried, trying to help, but actually hindering those who were carrying the wounded men on the stretcher or the tarpaulin. Some crossed both themselves and the soldiers.

The soldier who, five minutes before, had rushed out to meet the driver, barely managed to push his way through the crowd of women, and at the near end of the bridge, forgetting to turn out his forage-cap but none the less raising his hand to it in a salute, boldly declared: 'Comrade Major! Assault-group-leader Shkvaro and ten men reporting!'

The lieutenant's insignia were hidden under his fur collar, and, looking at Gavrilov's shabby coat, the soldier decided that the youthful commander in the new, immaculate sheepskin must be the senior of the two, if only by one rank.

'Report the situation!' said the motorcyclist sullenly. 'And you wait there just now!' he shouted to the other soldiers, who had entrusted the wounded to the women and were about to come across the bridge.

Private Shkvaro was lost for words, evidently expecting a different welcome.

'Where are your commanders?' asked the lieutenant.

'Gone,' said the soldier, lowering his eyes.

'What?' the lieutenant flared up.

Gavrilov gave a sigh at this display of temper, but refrained from interfering.

'They were killed,' said the soldier.

'Where have you come from?' asked the lieutenant crossly.

'Over there.' The soldier waved his hand in the direction of the woods.

'Put them in the church meanwhile,' said Gavrilov to the women who were carrying the wounded past him.

'I can see you've not come from Moscow!' roared the lieutenant. 'Are you from the forest? Did you break out of encirclement? Are you deserters?'

'Hold on, now,' Gavrilov interrupted him, at the same time wondering why he was getting involved, but losing his patience. 'Comrade soldier, how long is it since you were in action?'

'Two days.'

'You've been walking through the forest for two days?'

'We only walked in the forest at night.'

'And during the day over the fields, I suppose!' said the young lieutenant sarcastically.

'No, during the day we waited,' the soldier corrected him, understanding that one must not contradict commanders, that everything, even their sarcasm, had to be borne. 'We have five men wounded. Three cannot walk.'

'Yes, I saw,' Gavrilov nodded. 'How have you come? Give me the map,' he said, turning to the lieutenant.

'I can't. It's secret.'

'Ah . . . and mine is torn just at this spot . . . Have you been heading east all the time?' he asked the soldier.

'More or less . . .'

Gavrilov grinned good-humouredly. 'And you didn't meet any Germans?'

'No. We've been in the forest – we . . .'

'I told you they were running away!' said the motorcyclist gleefully.

'Just wait a minute!' Gavrilov cut him off again. 'Have you any weapons?'

'Yes, but not much. One Dyegtyaryov – and rifles, of course . . .'

'What about grenades?' asked Gavrilov, like an examiner prompting a pupil.

'Yes, grenades,' the soldier nodded, 'but not many, either.'

'Deserters,' said the dandy in the sheepskin morosely.

'Quit it,' Gavrilov chided him, thereby revealing his own seniority. 'Never mind lads,' he turned back to the soldier. 'It's all right. You'll get some food in you now. It's just a pity you know so little about the Germans. Didn't you even hear tanks?'

'I won't lie, Comrade Captain. We did hear them, but we didn't stick our heads out to see them. We were an assault group, you see – one and a half platoons. Both our lieutenants were killed. We were moving forward to join our company – when suddenly the Germans appeared, straight out of the blue. We beat them off twice, but this is all that was left of us. We escaped into the forest, and kept our heads down.'

'So there is fighting ahead?' Gavrilov sounded pleased.

'Yes, Comrade Captain,' said the soldier, also sounding pleased. 'All the time. There's thousands and thousands of our men out there, fighting like hell! It was pure chance that those Germans broke through. The tanks . . .'

'What else did you see?' asked Gavrilov.

'What else? Bombers,' Private Shkvaro shrugged.

'Hm, we've got enough of them here too,' Gavrilov grinned humourlessly. 'There they go again now.'

Above the forest, no more than six thousand feet up, three Junkers were flying, followed by two Messerschmidts, somewhat higher.

'Let's go, captain,' said the sheepskinned lieutenant quietly.

The soldier obediently remained at the bridge, while the women flocked towards the church, where a hubbub of voices filled the air: 'Have you seen Vanka Sizov?'

'Did you come across Sergei Yevteyev?'

'Listen, lads,' pleaded Ganya, overwrought, 'did you happen to meet the Shlykovs – Valentin and Valery Shlykov?'

'Well?' said Gavrilov, when he and the lieutenant reached the top of the hill.

'Will you remain here to take charge?' asked the lieutenant.

'What else would I do? Don't you see . . .' Gavrilov nodded to the church and the women.

'In that case don't interfere. Soldier, come here!' the lieutenant shouted down to the bridge.

'But just remember it's people you're dealing with,' said Gavrilov with a sigh, realizing he was wasting his breath.

'Don't try to teach me,' the lieutenant snarled back. 'Right, Comrade soldier,' he turned to the approaching Red Army man.' You've had your little walk in the woods, now you can do some fighting. These are your orders: dig yourselves rifle-pits on the other side of the bridge and take up defensive positions. When more men arrive you'll be relieved. Meanwhile – about turn! I'll have food brought to you.'

'Comrade Captain?' said the soldier, looking hopefully at Gavrilov: would he again contradict the young fellow in the sheepskin coat?

But Gavrilov merely asked: 'Do you need spades?'

'We could get the girls to help us!' smiled the soldier.

'Why not, indeed!' said the lieutenant cheerfully. 'There are plenty of them around!'

'You're not getting them,' said Gavrilov sullenly.

'What d'you mean?' The lieutenant sounded surprised.

'You're not getting them. Go and get spades, soldier, and send one of your men for porridge'. With that, the captain turned and walked to the church.

'What's this? Loath to part with your harem?' said Maria Ivanovna, who was standing nearby, as he passed her. 'I didn't think it was much use to you.'

'Well maybe it isn't, but it certainly won't do the women any good to cross that river.'

'Ah, don't panic, captain,' said the chief, running after him.

'Or was your commander's spirit castrated too?'

'Silly fool,' he smiled sadly. 'Poor unbearable silly fool that you are . . .'

'What are you going on about?'

'Nothing, Marusya, nothing . . . Listen: yesterday, on the phone, they promised a train. Believe it if you like, but be prepared to have to rely on ourselves. If . . .' he looked at the huge pocket-watch which he had converted into a wristwatch, 'if in forty minutes the wagons haven't arrived and there are no orders to the contrary, pack up and head back to town. An officer will meet you somewhere and tell you where to dig.'

'No-o!?' she breathed out in disbelief. 'And what's he up to?' She suddenly remembered about the lieutenant, who was now crossing the bridge to the other bank, behind the soldier.

'Get on your motorcycle!' Gavrilov shouted to him, but he merely waved his hand.

'He doesn't want to see the wounded men,' said the chief.

'No, no. He's just scared to ride out too far,' Gavrilov laughed, and gave Maria Ivanovna a slap on the bottom.

'What's this? Flirting now?' she said ironically.

'That's right. But unfortunately, Marusya, there's no time for flirting,' he said with a wink, knowing that they must now avoid a quarrel at all costs.

'So you were lying?'

'Well, what should I say . . . perhaps I embellished a little!'

'Well, well,' she shook her head. 'Quite an actor! Oh, look – here come your wagons!'

And sure enough, a grey cloud of smoke puffed up above the horizon, and there was a faint rumble of wheels in the distance.

13

'There's masses of rifles over there,' Goshka whispered to Liya when he returned from the bridge. Neither of them had relatives at the front, so they had not run off to see the wounded but had remained by their trench.

'It would be good if we could get one,' Liya nodded.

'The captain won't let us, damn him. That commander with the sub-machine-gun wanted to send women over the river, but the captain refused.' Goshka blushed, because he had kept to himself the reason why the lieutenant asked Gavrilov for the women. 'You see,' he added, trying to hide his embarrassment.

'Yes,' Liya agreed, although the tired and sullen captain inspired her with more confidence than the brave young motor-cyclist in the sheepskin.

'Do you know what, Liya,' Goshka said in a conspiratorial whisper, 'at a pinch we could cross over under the bridge at night. The water isn't so cold.'

'That's right,' Liya smiled.

'What are you whispering about?' shouted Sanka, coming down the hill. 'They haven't seen my old drunkard! He's probably all right, is Dad – bullets don't like alcoholics!'

'Shall we tell her?' asked Goshka indecisively. He liked the chubby, laughing girl.

'Let's ask her,' Liya whispered in agreement.

'Yes, why not!' exclaimed Sanka after they had explained their plan to her in an excited, noisy whisper. 'Except one Jerry's not enough. I'm not going to die for less than five of them!'

The cheerful lass did not actually want to die at all, and all this was just idle chatter for the time being.

'Oh, look, over there!' she suddenly exclaimed. 'Do you see? A train is coming this way.'

'I'm not going to call them together, captain. You do it,' grumbled Mara Ivanovna. 'I'm not a magician. I can't be everywhere at once.'

'All right. Hold on a minute,' said Gavrilov evasively.

The train was moving slowly. So far, only its smoke could be seen.

'That's everything under control!' announced the lieutenant, more cheerfully now, suddenly appearing behind Gavrilov's back. 'Girls, give the soldier here six bowls of porridge.'

Behind him stood a soldier in a dirty greatcoat, but with his cap now turned the right way round. Gavrilov could scarcely make out that this was a different man, not the one who had reported earlier.

'You turned back quickly,' he said to the lieutenant mockingly.

'So what? I've deployed the men. They're digging already.'

'You'll get a medal for that!'

'Quit the crap.'

'Why? You've stopped deserters. Eliminated panic. And set up defences. You could easily get a medal,' Gavrilov mocked. 'Give me a sheet of paper – I'll write a recommendation.'

'Well . . . I did stop them,' said the lieutenant, not very confidently.

'What about my part in it? Give me your binoculars, if they're not secret.'

Magnified six times, the puff of smoke moved no more quickly, but Gavrilov could see that the engine was again pushing three open goods-vans from behind. There were no people on them.

Suddenly Gavrilov remembered two lines from Mayakovsky's poem 'Ode to the Revolution', which one of the soldiers from the isolation ward had wanted to recite at the October Revolution celebrations in 1939:

> Sailors you send to a stinking ship
> To save a forgotten kitten . . .

'It's no use,' Gavrilov the political instructor had said, quite categorically.

The whole of the 'Lenin room', packed with thirty or more company performers, turned to look at him.

The poem contained other words, too, which Gavrilov found suspect, but he pounced on these particular ones.

'We didn't have a Revolution to save cats,' Gavrilov exploded.

'Did you take part in it yourself, Comrade Political Instructor?' asked the poetry-reader with a malicious look in his innocent little eyes.

'No. And neither did your Mayakovsky.'

'But he painted revolutionary posters.'

'Posters!' said Gavrilov scornfully.

Although he was a political instructor and, as it were, the patron of such amateur theatricals, he could not abide self-styled artists, and considered them slackers and simulators every one. A real soldier, he believed, was one who did not run away from service and did not ask his comrades to stand in for him on guard duty or kitchen duty. A real soldier – a real man, indeed – could have the whole company splitting their sides at his jokes and antics while on the march – without any rehearsals. But to recite something on the stage, whether from a piece or paper or from memory – any fool could do that.

But Gavrilov kept such thoughts to himself, because amateur theatricals were regarded as a great aid for commanders and political instructors in the task of strengthening military discipline, and so long as he was a political instructor he adhered to this view in public, and merely tried to repeat it as little as possible.

'Do you know,' the young recruit had objected, 'that "Mayakovsky is and remains the best and most talented poet"? Do you know who said that?'

'Yes, I know,' said Gavrilov.

'You see!' said the soldier, to the approval of all these layabouts from the theatrical circle. It was obvious that they didn't give a jot for their political instructor and were laughing in his face.

What a bunch of pedants and know-alls, he thought. He felt hurt not so much for his own sake as for the whole political corps of the Red Army.

'Let me see the book! Surely there are other poems in it. What about the one about the passport, or the garden-city?'

He took the thick volume, open at the first pages, glanced at the disputed poem, and immediately noticed the date below it: 1918.

'It's no use,' he handed the book back, feeling happier.

'May I appeal to the regimental commissar?' chirped the greenhorn.

'Oh, you can appeal,' scoffed Gavrilov, 'but he won't allow it either. Your Mayakovsky is from the Soviet period, but that poem is from the period of War Communism. There's a discrepancy, eh?'

And the unlucky performer was at last silenced – not exactly covered in shame, but lost for a suitable reply.

Maybe Mayakovksy was right after all, Gavrilov thought now, watching the three trucks and the engine through the binoculars. They're women, of course, not cats, but none the less they're being saved: they've sent transport even though there is such a shortage of it. What other country would do that? Then he also remembered the great rescue of the people on board the *Chelyuskin*, wrecked by ice-floes in 1934, and he became reconciled both with the young soldier, who was wounded on the second day of the war, and with Mayakovsky, who ended up shooting himself because of a woman.

'Here, take them,' he said, handing the binoculars back to the lieutenant, and now with the naked eye he could see a Messerschmidt looming out of the distance above the slowly moving train.

The railway embankment twisted to the right, and now the whole train could be seen from the church. It was backing away from the aeroplane, but the aeroplane swooped down on it. On its first run the Messerschmidt only fired a burst of machine-gun fire, then backed off sharply. The German fighter was tremendously fast, whereas the train was crawling along.

Now he'll give a blast from his guns, thought Gavrilov.

All over the hillside the women stood in awe, transfixed by the train and the fighter.

'Lie down!' Gavrilov shouted. 'Where are the wounded?' he asked, turning round, but they had already been taken inside the church. The lieutenant in the smart sheepskin was already flat on the ground, and the soldier who had come for porridge was also lying down, over beside the fire. On the hillside the women were jumping into the trenches. He'll go for the boiler now, thought Gavrilov, looking up from the ground as the plane began a large loop, positioning itself to fire from its guns at the lumbering train. Twenty-mil calibre. Should go straight through . . . Flying now directly above the railway line, the plane twice strafed the defenceless engine with shells, but they must have missed or ricocheted, for the train continued to lurch towards the bombed-out station.

'A-ha!' Gavrilov rejoiced, watching the fighter as it climbed a little and then began waggling its wings above the potato field. What's he bragging about? He hasn't killed the driver . . . thought the captain, turning his eyes back to the train, which was still slowly creeping on. No, he must be calling for support. Suddenly Gavrilov heard a rifle-shot. From the cabin of the truck, with his carbine resting on the open door, the student was aiming at the German plane.

It's a waste of time: he'll never hit it, thought the captain. Still, there's no harm: the pilot won't hear it over the engine noise.

And indeed, the Messerschmidt was still rocking its wings high above the field, as though nothing had happened.

Are you going or not, then? Gavrilov wondered nervously. Go

on, get lost. It's bad for me to lie on the ground, even if it is dry, he almost pleaded, as though it were a friendly plane, not a German one.

Suddenly, behind him, behind the church, there was a terrible roaring and whining like a factory siren. There were explosions, and the roofing iron started wailing, and then a huge yellow Junkers-87 bomber with a red nose and red wheels soared directly over Gavrilov's head.

This one was in no mood to play with the train like a well-fed cat with a mouse. Crossing the line at an acute angle, he dropped two bombs on the embankment. Gavrilov pressed his head to the ground, and before he even had time to realize that evacuation by train was now impossible, his ears were suddenly blocked by the whistle and crash of fresh explosions, and another enormous yellow bomber thundered over him, rather nearer to the railway embankment. The roar seemed to press on his head and neck, not allowing him to look round – and how he wanted to look round, to see what had happened on the hillside behind him.

The women . . . don't let them be hit! he prayed. His head was heavy and unreceptive of thoughts.

Behind the church there were two more bomb-blasts, and then machine-gun fire started up, cutting through the din of the sirens and the iron roof.

The wail spread all over the field, growing louder, then a little less, and then more deafening than ever.

What's the point of them fighting when there's no one to fight against? Gavrilov was thinking wearily, when suddenly a spray of earth from machine-gun fire erupted nearby. They must be attacking the other bank, he remembered, hearing new explosions coming fron the direction of the church.

'They're bombing your defences!' he shouted hoarsely to the lieutenant, but the lieutenant did not raise his head. 'You'll get used to it!' shouted the captain, but his words were lost in the growing howl of the Junkers as they came in low again. This time they overflew the hillside and the potato field, just missing the church, while the Messerschmidt, like a little brother, hung over them joyfully rocking its wings.

They're just trying to intimidate us with noise, Gavrilov reflected, slowly growing accustomed to the siren-like whining. They're certainly not wasting cartridges. But that was just tempting Providence: immediately another burst of fire spurted over the ground, and as the roar receded there was a crash of glass.

They've got the truck, he thought, and turned to look, shielding his eyes with his hand. The windscreen was gone, but the student was alive, because the barrel of his carbine was still aiming above the top of the door.

Bloody hell! He's got guts, anyway! the captain thought, trying to smile. 'Hey, take a leaf out of our lad's book!' he shouted to the lieutenant, who remained, however, with his head firmly down on the damp ground.

From the slope the railway embankment could not be seen so clearly, but even from there the women closely followed the train and its attacker. None of them knew it had been sent for them, and they simply felt sorry for it since it could do nothing to escape from its vulnerable position. The train approached the hill, with the plane descending upon it, and when the first attack failed the women felt overjoyed for an instant – until they realized that, with the station destroyed, there would be no escape for the train anyhow. The plane soared off into the sky, then returned, and opened fire, but the train still trundled on and on towards the station.

On the hillside they cheered and started waving their arms: 'Turn back! Turn back!' But the driver either did not hear, or was afraid to stop, and the engine moved remorselessly towards the smashed section of the line. Now they had a good view of it from the hillside, but just then the Junkers appeared, and nobody dared to look up at what followed. Bombs began to fall, and those women who had time scrambled into the trenches, while the others buried their heads in the earth of the slope.

At first the bombs fell on the embankment, then on the other bank, and two dropped into the river, sending a fountain of water over Goshka, who was lying above his first trench, not having managed to jump into it. The roar of the aircraft seemed to pass over Goshka in slow motion, crushing his back as though a tank or a caterpillar-tractor were grinding over it. His stomach churned, and its contents – hot, sour porridge – gushed up to his nose and ears and spewed out through his mouth on to the soft damp earth of the parapet. Goshka could not raise his head, and the vomit, mixed with mud, ran down his cheeks.

Shells seemed to be criss-crossing the whole slope, and Goshka felt as if they were aiming at him alone, trying to pin him for ever to the sticky mud, but somehow kept missing. Again the din would drown everything, and he would be consumed with pain as though a tooth were being extracted without anaesthetic – or rather, a though his whole body were being pulled out of somewhere against his will.

He spluttered and coughed as he threw up again and the vomit got into his eyes. He lay hating himself, and, losing strength, he called out: 'Mother! Mu-u-um!' Over the noise of the bombers, nobody, thank God, could hear him. 'O-oh, I'm going to be killed,' he groaned, feeling that if he was sick again his heart and lungs would come up too. 'Ah. What the . . . I must . . . I must . . .' he whispered, immediately forgetting what it was he must do. Whenever the roar died down a little he remembered that he must shoot at the planes – but he had nothing to shoot with, and he cursed the captain. Suddenly the thunderous roar returned, and little fountains of mud sprayed over him again. 'The captain, the bastard . . . didn't let me . . . the captain . . . he didn't let me . . . the bastard . . .' he kept repeating like a prayer, with his bespattered eyes tight shut. The whole bank was pitted with gunfire, and from the ground only faint moans went up in reply. The Degtyaryov on the other bank was also silent: evidently there was no one left alive over there.

Liya was lying twenty yards up from Goshka in the trench they had just begun. There was nowhere for her to hide, and when she opened her eyes briefly she saw three planes flying overhead – two big and one small.

Oh my God . . . She covered her head with her hands. Imagine dying for nothing. For nothing, for nothing . . . And do nothing about it. Where are *our* planes? Where are they? I'll be killed any minute now. We all will! Her heart pounded inside her, and the planes howled overhead.

She did not know where to hide her head, which suddenly seemed not to belong to her, and felt huge and heavy and clumsy. Through the aircraft noise she heard Yelena Fedotovna's mournful voice: 'There is no one for us to rely on.'

You must keep sane! Liya checked herself and opened her eyes. The church was still standing, and behind it she could just see the truck, behind the door of which a rifle barrel was peeping out. The rifle was moving along the top of the door, then it jerked, and then slowly moved back again.

It's that boy! Well done . . . ! Liya realized. And I'm doing nothing . . . nothing . . .

'Never mind, it's all right,' another quiet but persistent voice tried to reassure her. The voice came from far, far away, knocking in her head like the wheels of an approaching train.

They haven't sent a train, she thought, but just then caught sight of the engine with its three goods-vans, standing motionless on the track not far from the line of the trenches, in front of her and to the right. There were intermittent puffs of steam coming from its funnel. The driver must be dead, Liya decided. Then the aircraft roared past again and deafened her for a moment.

'It's all right . . .' The voice knocked in her head, moving from the back of her neck to her ears and temples, while overhead droned the aeroplanes, which the truck-driver was still unable to hit.

Sanka and Ganya were among the first to manage to jump into a trench, and now they lay right at the bottom. The bomb-blasts caused the sides of the trench to crumble, and the earth got under their kerchiefs, into their ears and hair. Both were terrified, but each in her own way. Ganya shook with terror, but Sanka felt anguished – so anguished that her body, normally so healthy and full of life, turned sickly and numbed. I'm like Liya's old witch, she thought – or rather, somehow felt.

Now I'll be killed, and there will be nothing left. I'll be buried here. For some reason she imagined herself being stripped, and her white sides and breasts being covered in this damp earth full of slithering worms, and she was seized by such fear that she was ready to jump out of the trench and expose herself to the screaming German planes. The slimy earth frightened her more than the yellow dragons in the sky. But there were two more women on top of her, and she did not dare even to disturb them, far less throw them off, so paralysed did she feel inside . . .

'Viktor. Viktor!' Sanka screamed inwardly, not knowing who else to call for help. 'You were the only one I had . . .' The words echoed in her head, which felt crushed by the crumbling earth, the women, and the aircraft noise.

Ganya lay totally stunned until the planes flew away, like a chicken grown tired of flapping in the hands of a cook before dinner.

14

'Get up!' said Gavrilov to the lieutenant. 'They've gone. Do you hear?!' He no longer had the strength to make fun of him. 'Get up,' he repeated sadly. 'You'll have to report to headquarters.'

The lieutenant still lay there. Gavrilov bent over him and shook his shoulder; he was lying as though dead.

Gavrilov lifted the lieutenant's head. His eyes were closed, and his head slowly slipped over Gavrilov's palm and struck the jacket of his sub-machine-gun.

He's had it! thought the captain, and only then did he notice two neat little holes in his sheepskin coat, barely any larger than the holes made by a paper-puncher.

He won't do much more commanding! sighed the captain, feeling nothing, as his head was still reverberating with the bomb explosions, the roaring, and the gap of gunfire. He left the dead man and went to the church.

'Student! Are you alive?' he cried, starting at the sound of his own voice.

'Yes. I missed them all,' replied the truck-driver gloomily, as though he and the captain were at the regimental shooting ground.

'Good lad!' Gavrilov wanted to say, but his voice was choked with tears. He managed to get the words out very quietly, and then went up to the truck. The sides were all dented and scraped, as though a gang of youths had attacked it with nails and knives or broken glass. The sides of the cabin were covered in bullet holes and pock-marks. The windscreen was gone, but the radiator was safe, and the engine was already going.

'Looks like we survived!' the student grinned. 'Shall I round up the wounded?'

'Yes!' said Gavrilov, wiping mud from his forehead. 'Let's collect them. Will you do it? Well done, student! Not like . . .' He was about to say something about the lieutenant, until he remembered he was dead. 'Yes, we must bring in the wounded. You see to it . . .' He walked away to where the fire had been.

All around people were slowly beginning to get up and move about, dusting themselves down, and even talking, but he saw and heard everything almost as if through a shroud or through water. They looked like drowned people to him.

He caught sight of Maria Ivanovna, standing over two women who were lying on the ground. But at first he did not see the women.

'You're alive, Maria Ivanovna? Your man isn't.'

'Neither is yours,' said the women's commander, with a nod towards the soldier, who was lying about ten yards from the dead women. His bowls of porridge were scattered round him, cold. 'And he died hungry,' sighed Maria Ivanovna.

'Get his papers from his pocket. The driver will hand them in,' said Gavrilov, trying to turn away as quickly as possible from the dead women. 'You'll have to get everybody ready, my dear.' He suddenly embraced her in front of everyone, but then pushed her away again and walked down the slope.

'Any wounded?' he called, hurrying along the trenches. 'Any wounded here?'

'Further on, I think,' said the women, clambering out of their holes.

Catching sight of Sanka, he asked her to go and check. 'Are you all right?' he asked Liya, who was sitting in her trench. She nodded, without getting up.

'Is your lad alive?' asked Gavrilov, remembering Goshka.

Liya indicated the river with a flick of her head. Goshka was there, squatting, and washing his face.

'Right,' the captain sighed. 'Get everyone together and come to the church. We're leaving.' He turned and strode quickly back to the lieutenant.

'I'm afraid I have to disturb you,' he said, removing his submachine-gun and binoculars. 'Ah, and his map and documents,' he remembered. He turned him over carefully, unbuttoned his coat, and took his Party card and identity card from the pocket of his field-shirt. 'Alexei Stepanovich Gavrilkin,' he read. 'Look at that, he's almost my namesake,' he thought, squinting at the dead man as he pocketed the documents and attached the second map-case to his belt. 'Excuse me,' he mumbled, his thoughts preoccupied with the living. 'Oh, yes, you had wheels too, didn't you!'

The lieutenant's motorcycle, with its antler-like handlebars, was still propped against the side of the church.

So what next then? Evacuation? Looks like it . . . Gavrilov debated with himself as he walked back to the trenches.

'Come and help carry the wounded!' he shouted. 'And quickly!'

'Give the driver his papers,' he said to Maria Ivanovna, who was kneeling over the dead soldier.

'Hey,' he shouted down to Goshka. 'Come here.'

Goshka trotted up the hill.

'Go and get the machine-gun. You're going to Moscow,' grinned Gavrilov, deciding that the motorcycle and the gun would be too much for one man. 'Go on – what are you waiting for?' he added, taking Goshka's dazed look for shyness. 'Pick it up and go and join the driver.'

At least he's still alive, he thought languidly. He's still got some fighting ahead of him . . .

'Any wounded here?' he shouted again, hurrying along the slope.

'Here!'

'Take them to the truck.'

He did not want to look at the wounded women.

'How many dead are there?' he asked when he got back to the women's commander.

'Only two so far. Both cooks.'

'Take a note of their names and have them buried in a trench. And quickly. We must leave. The tanks could come any minute.'

'What are *they* doing?' she pointed to the other bank. 'Or are they . . .' And she imitated the sound of falling bombs.

'I don't know,' he frowned. 'You look after your girls.'

He had tended to push the soldiers on the other bank to the back of his mind. All he was concerned about were the women and the wounded in the church.

'Tell everybody we're leaving. They should take their spades, but never mind the picks. And tell them to fill their bags with the food that's there – there's some groats, and sugar left. And see that they don't all crowd together on the road like sheep – it would be dangerous if *they* come back . . .' He glanced at the sky, but there were many clouds about now, as though driven in by the aeroplanes. It was quickly growing dark.

'Ow! Don't drop me,' groaned a woman who was being carried away by three others.

'Put her in the truck,' said the captain, turning round.

'Are there many wounded?' he shouted in the direction of the trenches, but received no answer.

'All right . . . Listen, Maria Ivanovna. You take them to Moscow, and I'll check here.' He went to try out the motorcycle, and it started up at once.

'It's got a full tank. I looked,' said the driver.

'I'll just go and check there's no one left in the trenches,' said Gavrilov, almost apologizing to the student for everything – for the bombing, the wounded women, the damaged truck, and now for this unexpectedly acquired trophy.

'The women don't need us now. We'll only cause them trouble now.'

'That's right,' the student nodded.

'Drive the truck out on to the road. They'll bring the wounded there. Otherwise . . .' He looked up at the sky again. The clouds were darkening fast. 'Good luck, anyway!' He held out his hand to the driver. 'Take the lad with you,' he said, pointing at Goshka, who was sitting in the cabin with the machine-gun against his chest. 'Oh, and take these papers. He's almost got the same name as mine. Give them to the first person you meet, whoever it is. And in general, report everything that happened . . .'

'What about you?' asked the driver.

'I'll get away somehow,' said Gavrilov, patting the fuel-tank of the motorcycle. 'Or if the worst comes to the worst, I've enough here, too.' He adjusted the holster of his revolver.

The women were already stretching out along the main road from the church. They walked gloomily, as though from a funeral. Their bags swung from the spades over their shoulders, and the buckets in their hands were so heavy they scarcely squeaked. Gavrilov drove past them and turned off to the bridge. The motorcycle warmed him, and the quivering pedal did not bother his wounded leg. On the contrary, it even soothed it. Gavrilov felt a little happier.

Suddenly a voice rang out from the right side of the road: 'Comrade Commander!' He braked and came to a halt just above the home-made anti-tank barriers in the ditch. The old man, in a soft cap with a cloth peak, and wrapped in his long raincoat, climbed out of a half-dug trench. Gavrilov smiled to himself: he had clean forgotten about him.

'What is it, Granddad?' he asked.

'Well, from my understanding of things, the barriers aren't needed any more?' said the old man. His three young lads were sitting on a parapet behind his back.

'Are they all safe?' asked Gavrilov, indicating the boys.

'Yes,' said the old man through clenched teeth. 'So the barriers won't be needed now? Is that the case?' He waved his hand at the women who were walking away in the opposite direction.

'Yes, forget it, Granddad,' said Gavrilov with a sigh.

'There's nothing for me to forget,' said the old man, becoming agitated. 'It's you that's forgetting me, not the other way round.' And, looking through his spectacles, which were tied together with bits of string, at the exhausted, unshaven captain, he added with malice: 'They put up a better show than this in Karelia.'

'It was winter there,' said Gavrilov quietly, and started wheeling his motorcycle away, ashamed to get on to the saddle in front of the old man.

'So I should wait for winter, should I?' he shouted after Gavrilov in a thin voice. 'There's your winter . . . !' He flourished his hand at the low, thick black clouds.

Gavrilov did not look round, but wheeled his motorcycle down from the road to the riverbank, and drove off along the water's edge towards the railway bridge.

'Any wounded here?' he shouted.

The last women were leaving the trenches and walking up to the road. Some of them were snatching a moment to wash their faces in the river.

'Come on – no time for that!' Gavrilov sent them away.

They obediently got up and traipsed after the others. Gavrilov drove along the bank as far as the embankment, then about twenty yards along the embankment, and finally turned and drove up the other side of the hill to the church. He tried not to think about the train, which now stood silently rooted to the rails, or about the driver and stoker. They were about a mile from the church, and it was simply beyond his strength to order the women to go and drag the dead men from the engine.

'Any wounded?' he cried again.

Maria Ivanovna and three other women were hurriedly burying the dead women not far from the church.

'Go now, Maria Ivanovna. I'll finish it. Go on,' said the captain.

'There's still those two,' replied the squad-leader, nodding at the soldier and the lieutenant, who were lying on the breastwork of a trench, and whom she could not bring herself to bury together with the cooks. 'He's got a good coat,' she added, looking at the lieutenant.

'Go on,' said Gavrilov. 'Catch up with your girls. And if tanks do appear, tell them to get rid of their spades at once.'

'How will you get away?'

'I've got wheels.'

'Will you catch us up?'

'No.' He shook his cap. 'Goodbye. We never did have our fun, did we?'

'Never mind. We may meet again,' she grinned. 'Here, take this spade. Come on, girls,' she called to the women and led them away.

'Stop!' he almost shouted after her, noticing that the dead officer's sheepskin coat, but had second thoughts. 'Ah, maybe not. I've dispossessed him as it is.'

He got down into the trench and carefully pulled the dead men into it by their shoulders – first the soldier, then the lieutenant – trying to position them neatly.

'Well, there's a thing!' Gavrilov remembered the lieutenant's words. 'They've turned blue!' he said aloud. 'And one way or another, I'm going to cop it, too!' And clambering out of the trench, he started filling in the grave with earth from the parapet. I'll let the women at least reach the junction; then I'll take the road to the post office . . . Being fit and to all appearances uninjured, he did not wish to ride past the women, trudging along the road exhausted by the digging and the bombing, on a motorcycle.

What use was I to them anyway? he continued arguing with himself. They didn't even need your porridge: they could just have baked potatoes! His temples started humming, and his neck aching, from all he had seen. A hundred kilometres for five sacks of millet . . . I don't know about porridge, but we're certainly in a stew! He tried to laugh it off, but the joke sounded false. When we didn't find engineers here, we should have left on foot, and that would have been that. The old man wouldn't have kept them back

. . . He remembered the round little man in the trenchcoat with annoyance. Ah, who knows what was best . . .

Still, this is no time to get angry, he said to himself. I must go for the receipt.

He quickly filled in the rest of the grave, leaving it slightly raised above the ground. Then he took an indelible pencil from his map-case, wet it in his mouth, and wrote on the haft of his spade:

TWO MOSCOW WOMEN
Lt. GAVRILKIN

Damn it, he thought. I've forgotten his first name.

He did not know even the surname of the soldier, so he added merely:

A RED ARMY SOLDIER

Just then he heard the sound – barely audible – of whimpering or sobbing. 'Who's there?' he cried.

The sobbing grew louder.

'Where are you?' the captain asked anxiously.

'In the church . . .' said a female voice.

Gavrilov ran into the church. In a dark corner, near the sacristy, a woman sat huddled up in a padded jacket and ski-pants.

'What is it? Are you wounded?' Gavrilov asked fearfully, since the truck was gone.

'No,' replied Sanka, shaking her head, and continuing to whimper.

15

The student had driven the truck out on to the road and waited for the last wounded women to be brought in.

'Is that everyone?' he shouted into the darkness as he closed the back of the truck. There were nineteen wounded in all – five men and fourteen women.

Ganya, who had been lingering near the truck, started whining again: 'Take me, will you, lad? I'm in as bad a state as any of them, worse in fact.'

'Oh, what the hell – get in, missus!' the student agreed. 'Leave your spade. Here, stand on the back wheel and jump over. And be quick, otherwise . . .'

He was afraid some of the other women would ask, too, but they all trooped past in silence, quite unlike the cheerful crowd who had filled the station yard the day before.

'I really ought to give the redhead a lift – she's got no strength at all,' thought the student, and looked around, but Liya was nowhere to be seen.

He also fancied taking on board some of the girl students who had been digging over by the embankment, but the very thought embarrassed him and he drove it away. Those girls were young: they would make it on foot.

'Has anybody any cartridges left?' he asked the soldiers in the truck. 'I've used up all of mine.'

'Here,' replied a voice inside, and a hand reached out with a belt and two leather cartridge pouches.

'Fine! Let's get going!' said the student as he got into the cabin. 'Only, point that thing the other way,' he said to Goshka, nodding at the machine-gun. 'Or better still, let me take out the drum.'

He pulled back the catch, and to Goshka's displeasure placed the magazine next to him on the seat. The truck moved off, and with the wind blowing straight in it became very cold.

'Brrr – goes right through you,' said the student. 'You have a broader sector of fire, though!' He pointed at the empty wind-screen-frame. 'You're baptized now, eh?'

'What?' shouted Goshka. He could hear nothing for the wind.

'Were you scared?' the driver shouted.

Goshka shrugged his shoulders. The truck accelerated, and the most one could do against the cold was to cover one's face with one's sleeve.

'So was I!' the driver yelled back. 'My hands were shaking. I'd never been caught in an air-raid before.'

Goshka could not make out the words, but he nodded in agreement.

'Where's the redhead?' shouted the driver.

Goshka nodded again. He had not heard properly.

'Where's the red-haired girl?' the driver roared into his ear.

'I don't know,' cried Goshka, shielding his voice from the wind with his hand.

'Is she alive?'

'Yes, yes.'

He did not know how to tell the driver about Liya. The wind was blowing furiously, and immediately beyond the junction they encountered snow – or, rather, hard, fine hailstones.

Liya he had seen for the last time as he ran to the truck with the machine-gun. He even thought he heard her call him but he had no time to talk with her, and it would have been awkward in the presence of the captain who had detailed him for such an important task. Besides, he had forgotten about all their earlier plans and ideas. During the air-raid they had just flown out of his head, and afterwards he was occupied with the wounded. They won't leave her behind, he thought now to comfort himself. Meanwhile, out of solidarity with the driver, he tried not to shield his face too much from the driven hailstones. With his right hand he stroked the gun, with his left the magazine drum on the seat. The hail was battering his face, and it was impossible to ask the driver to go more slowly. He tried not to think about what had happened to him during the bombing.

Liya had seen Goshka running up to the captain, and realized that he would not come back, but she was not unduly distressed. Their conversations before the air-raid were like a far-off childhood, and now the real moment was approaching – the last, decisive moment, which she must not miss or let slip. 'Goshka is just a little boy,' she smiled wryly, remembering his face – greenish and not properly washed, worn out and suffering, but happy – and his thin little neck with a tommy-gun dangling from it . . . I'll ask Sanka. If she doesn't want to, I'll go alone. They're fighting out there. That's the front line, and if I arrive with a rifle they are hardly likely to send me away. I may not even have far to go since the Germans have broken through somewhere. It's a pity I don't know those girls who were singing on the train. I could have persuaded them to come with me. But they weren't digging anywhere near the bridge and didn't hear what the Red Army man said.

She looked over at the embankment, but the jolly girls were gone. Presumably they were already on the highway.

Well, too bad. I'll go myself if Sanka refuses. I'll find plenty of other soldiers out there.

'Yes, I'm all right,' she said to the captain, as he walked gloomily past her little trench for the second time. Thank God, I'm not wounded, her thoughts went on. But even if I was, I would stay . . . 'If a friend is wounded . . .' – Ah, songs . . . It's not like that at all. There must be a lot of weapons across the river. Wounded men, too, probably. But that's the captain's job – to bring in the wounded. I'll just get a gun – a rifle. What a shame we weren't taught how to use a light machine-gun . . .

Her eyes followed the captain, who suddenly changed direction and returned to the church instead of going to the bridge.

I'll have to hide from him. What if there are wounded men over the bridge? Maybe I should ask the old man? He could take them into the village on his wheelbarrow and hide them in an attic or cellar . . . But no – it's disgraceful! Why doesn't the captain go for those men?!

She tried to get up, but her legs were like jelly.

Never mind, I'll wait for a while – until the women are all away. But the captain really ought to go and pick up those soldiers on the other bank. Perhaps the driver will go for them – what a hero he was! He kept firing while everyone else was terrified. It would be better if he would stay, and let the captain drive the wounded to hospital . . .

'What are you hanging about here for?' asked Sanka, bending over her. 'You'll catch cold.'

'I'm all right,' said Liya with a faint smile. 'I'm just waiting . . . We agreed – have you forgotten?'

'What – you mean the rifles? Forget it! Let me help you up.'

'Suit yourself.'

'Let's go to the church and pick up our bag and pail. We can fill them with sugar.'

'You go on,' said Liya. She could hardly move her legs.

The other women were quickly leaving the slope, some of them carrying their wounded comrades, who were groaning with pain. Near the church wall, where the rearmost trench had been dug, lay the two dead cooks. The commander in the sheepskin coat and the soldier who had come for porridge were also dragged there like logs.

'Nice coat!' said Sanka, pointing to the lieutenant. Then she turned to Liya: 'I'm not letting you go.'

'You go on,' replied Liya. 'Kill your five Germans in Moscow.'

'Just you wait!' said Sanka, losing her temper. 'Maria Ivanovna!' she called, but not quite loudly enough for her to hear. 'I'm going to report you . . .'

'You would do that, would you?!' hissed Liya in a voice not her own. The two girls stood opposite one another – the one tall and imposing, the other small and thin – ready to lay hands upon each other.

Sanka was the first to cool down: 'You fool. Look at yourself. What can you do? Kick sand in their faces? Didn't you see what it was like just now?'

'There are guns over the river,' Liya repeated stubbornly.

There were guns over the river, and beyond that the front line, and Liya knew there would not be another chance like this to join the army. She would never have forgiven herself afterwards if she had yielded to Sanka now. Perhaps if she really insisted in Moscow, Sanka would manage to get into the army, because she was strong and fit. But Liya – thin, weak, and sickly-looking – would certainly be rejected. No, the last and only chance for her to register as a volunteer would be if she turned up with a rifle at the field of battle.

'I'm going. Goodbye,' she told her friend with an arrogant nod, and, scarcely able to drag her feet, turned to leave.

Sanka grabbed her by the shoulder: 'Wait!'

'Any wounded here? Come on, get moving, quickly!' shouted the captain from his motorcycle. He was riding along the riverbank, chasing away the women who were washing before setting out on their long trek.

'Go!' said Liya.

The captain rode on towards the railway bridge. Darkness was falling quickly and the two girls were almost alone already.

'I shan't let you.' Sanka suddenly broke down in tears.

'Let's go together, then.'

'No, there's dead men over there,' Sanka whined. 'I'm scared of them . . .' Now she was wailing like her kindergarten charges.

'Go to Moscow,' replied Liya, good-natured but tired.

'No.' Sanka shook her head.

'Go on.'

The noise of the motorcycle approached again: the captain was returning on the other side of the slope.

'He'll spot us!' Sanka sighed hopefully.

'Get down!' Liya breathed, and started stumbling towards the bridge.

'Will you come back?' Sanka called after her. 'I'll wait for you in the church.'

'Don't bother,' shouted Liya, almost certain that her friend would stay behind.

She dragged herself across the bridge. It was dark and scary. To the right of the bridge the old man in the trenchcoat and his three boys were walking along the bank.

I should call to them, thought Liya, in case there are wounded men here. But she did not call, fearing that the captain might hear.

She saw the first dead soldier immediately beyond the bridge on the cobbled road, which an explosion had turned into a shambles. He was buried up to his chest in a crater, still gripping the broken handle of a spade.

'Comrade!' she said, bending over him and touching his shoulder. He turned round submissively – too easily, somehow – and Liya suddenly saw that he was not buried at all, but severed at the waist.

She let out a little scream, and started shaking, but tried to force herself to stop, and bit her lip until it bled. Inside, she trembled madly, as though the bombing was starting up again.

Without looking round, she ran into the forest. Here it was even darker.

'Are there . . . are there . . . any wounded?' she panted, her heart beating like a drum-stick.

She staggered and struck her head against a birch tree, put her arms round it and clung to it, and could not tear herself away from the trunk.

At last she asked in a graveyard whisper: 'Are there any wounded?' Nobody replied. Only Sanka's voice could be heard, faintly, coming from the other bank: 'Liya! Liya!' But Liya had no strength to answer.

16

'What are you hiding here for?' Gavrilov asked sternly. 'Waiting for the Germans, or what?'

'Germans! I'm waiting for my friend,' Sanka sobbed. 'She went to get the rifles.'

'What? Which rifles?'

'The rifles on the other bank.'

'Get out of here,' said Gavrilov angrily, thinking: 'Why do they all keep going on at me about that other bank?' 'Come on. Get out of here,' he repeated. 'There's nobody there. I chased them all away from the river.'

'You're lying!' said Sanka, feeling slightly less unhappy.

'I'm not Goebbels! Come on . . . Well, where is she, your friend?' he asked, once Sanka had picked up her bag and followed him outside. It was pitch-dark and cold, with prickly hailstones pouring down.

'You see, there's nobody there.'

'Liya!' Sanka called out. 'No, she crossed the river . . . Li-ya!' she yelled again. 'Liya! I've got her documents, and we have only one bag between us. Li-ya!'

Only the whistling wind replied. It was becoming rather frightening in the empty black and white field.

'Liya! Lii-yaah!' The words rang out over the woods. 'What can I do?' Sanka wailed.

'Run and get her. I'll give you five minutes.'

'No – I'm scared,' said Sanka in a frightened whisper. 'I'm scared to go over there . . . Liya! Liya!!'

'She can't be there,' said Gavrilov as surely as possible. 'I didn't allow anyone to cross the bridge.' Then he shouted himself: 'Liya!'

'Let's go together,' she said, taking Gavrilov's arm.

'No,' he said firmly, freeing his arm. Meanwhile he strained to listen in the darkness for signs of any wounded who might remain. But nobody was groaning, or if they were, too quietly to be heard. 'No,' he said harshly, 'I'm not going over there. And she isn't there either. She left with the others.'

'What will I do?' said Sanka, sniffing.

'Get on the pillion: I'll take you as far as the road junction. Hold these binoculars for me. And put your bag under you, or it will hurt.'

'Li-i-ya!' cried Sanka for the last time from the motorcycle. There was no response.

'Hold tight,' said Gavrilov, and the motorcycle lurched forward and headed down to the road.

There was now a proper blizzard blowing. The snow darted through the blue headlight, and the two riders felt chilled not merely by the cold and the sharp wind, but by a feeling of apprehension.

It's like the next world, thought Gavrilov. And if I'm not careful that's where I'll end up . . . He no longer remembered about the Germans, as if the warm girl behind him were shielding him from them, and kept his eyes firmly on the road. Nothing was visible in the whiteness, and he was afraid of missing the turn-off. But soon the little cabin and the raised barrier came into view.

'Are you getting off?' said the captain, braking. 'The others are somewhere along that road. They can't have got far.'

'No, no,' said Sanka, pressing up to him and not loosening her grip on his coat.

'Is it painful?'

'I'll survive!'

'Grit your teeth, then. It'll be even bumpier now.'

'You should have taken that sheepskin,' Sanka breathed into Gavrilov's ear, as though she had been listening to his thoughts.

'He's colder than I am,' he joked in bad taste. Sanka hugged him with both arms and squeezed even tighter then before.

Well, now I'm sitting pretty, he thought. Operation successfully completed . . . I'll get mentioned in the dispatches! The poor girl will be shaken to bits – he altered his train of thought and smiled, so far as the wind and the hard stinging snow would allow him. I just hope that telephonist hasn't lost the receipt . . . Perhaps I'll phone again and explain . . . The girl is certainly keeping my back warm! he thought gratefully again about Sanka.

'Frozen?' he asked, looking round. His cap-strap dug into his cheek.

'No,' she replied, moving her breasts against his back. He felt this clearly through his coat and her wadded jacket.

'Be patient. We'll soon be there. We've to go to the post office.'

He felt like speaking with her. The snow was now blowing from the right and was less of a problem. On the hill, just as they were entering the village, the motorcycle shuddered twice, but the captain kept control of the machine and searched for the post office, following the dark wires in the white flying snow.

Again it was locked and there was no light in the window. Gavrilov knocked on the door, swore, and then, seeing the padlock, remembered that the key ought to be under the railing. Indeed it was, and Gavrilov opened the door.

Through the snowstorm Sanka, who was still sitting on the pillion, looked orphaned and abandoned. He shouted to her from the porch in mock Polish: 'Come in, miss. Make yourself at home. I'll be back soon – I'm not going far.'

The third cottage from the end was also dark. Gavrilov pushed open the front door, then another, walked straight into a table in the darkness, and cursed in no uncertain manner.

'Is there anyone alive in here?'

'Whaddaye want?' wheezed a disgruntled, drunken voice in the corner.

'The telegraphist.'

'She's not 'ere. She's gone to the district . . . The line's broken somewhere.'

'Damn it!' Gavrilov sighed, then went out to his motorcycle and followed his track in the snow back to the post office. There, he got off and stood for a moment in the porch looking at the driving snow. With a decisive gesture of his hand, he then went back out and pulled the motorcycle up the steps of the porch.

'It's like a primus stove: it will be warmer with it in here,' he said to Sanka, but then turned the engine off, remembering that exhaust fumes can be lethal.

Sanka was squatting in front of the Dutch stove.

'Ah! You've lit it already!' he said with a mixture of surprise and pleasure.

'Yes, everything was ready there,' she said.

Gavrilov looked round the room. With the stove crackling, and the lamp burning, he did not feel like leaving. And where could I go on a night like this? he asked himself. The Germans are also human – they won't poke their noses out till morning. If the worst comes to the worst, the girl should be all right, and I'll fight them off . . . Why should I risk my life in such weather, with this hole in my lung? The doctor warned me against catching a chill . . .

'Let's try out the blower, shall we?' he said aloud, to drive away his thoughts, and turned the telephone-handle three times. The receiver was silent. Then he turned the handle again without replacing the receiver. He heard a crackle, and then the line went quiet again.

'There was a safe somewhere. I must try it,' he said. 'Are you thawing out?' he asked Sanka. 'Don't burn your feet!'

Sanka was sitting with her boots off and her ski-pants pulled up, holding her stockinged feet almost inside the stove.

'You're very concerned!' she retorted without turning round.

'I used to be, lass, I used to be! Right now I'm concerned with this safe,' he said, slapping the side of the small filing cabinet. 'I'm not in the habit of breaking into safes, but what the hell!'

Even using a spanner which he found in the motorcycle pouch, the lock would not give. The cabinet slid about on the floor.

'Come here, will you,' he called to Sanka. 'They can have you too, for complicity! Sit on top of the cabinet . . . There . . . That's a bit better.' He placed the spanner on top of the padlock, and hit it hard with a log. The first time it did not work. 'You're too hot. You're distracting me!' he joked. At the second blow, however, the padlock flew off, together with the ring on the cabinet.

Apart from Gavrilov's ten-rouble note, the cabinet contained a few threes and single-rouble notes, and some long thin booklets of receipts. There were also two bottles – one full, the other half-emptied by the driver the day before. It's a wonder he didn't crash, thought Gavrilov.

He took the booklets into the lamplight, and sure enough, his receipt was neatly pinned to one of them. 'You're in luck, Political Instructor!' he whistled. 'Well, in for a penny, in for a pound: fancy a warmer-upper?'

'I wouldn't mind!' replied Sanka from beside the stove.

'Pity there's nothing to eat with it. Hang on, though – have a look in the cupboard. We'll pay for everything together.'

What do I need money for, he said to himself, angrily and bitterly. I can't even send my dependants' allowance out; their post office will be as useless as this one. He glanced at the telephone, and picked up the receiver again: 'Hello? Hello! All right, please yourself. I don't need you that much!'

'You're in a good mood,' laughed Sanka. 'There's some *sauerkraut* here, and potatoes. We could bake them.'

'Excellent!' He felt somewhat cheerier. The stove was crackling, there was no hail blowing in his face, the receipt for the phone call was in his pocket, and Sanka was already setting the table.

If they need me, they'll wake me, he said to himself, sitting down on the trestle-bed, which was covered with a thick grey blanket. And as he watched Sanka bustling at the table he knew, as surely as a domino player with all the right dominoes in his hands, exactly how the game would turn out now.

'Are there any wounded here?' Liya shouted again. Suddenly the wind got up, and the cold sharp hailstones swept down from the black sky.

I'll never see the rifles, she thought, and overcoming her fear, tried to hobble back to the crater. With horror she remembered the dead soldier and decided she must bury him. But she could not see any spades. She scrambled round the shell-crater, but slipped and fell into another one, at the side of the road, containing cobble-stones scattered by the explosion. Trying to clamber out of this second crater, she struck her knee painfully against an upturned machine-gun support.

Almost crying with pain, she tried to calm herself: No no, there must be rifles here . . . First I'll find a rifle, then I'll come back and bury the soldier.

But a voice inside her told her: 'You won't come back.'

'Word of honour . . . Komsomol's honour!' she cried aloud, groping her way between the wood and the riverbank . . . She saw something black on a tree, and froze. Then she discerned that it was a Red Army greatcoat hanging on the branches, turned out like a sail.

It must have been blown up there by the blast,' she said loudly. 'They would have taken their coats off to dig . . .' She shuddered, remembering that the dead soldier was also only wearing a field-shirt.

'Is anybody wounded?' she cried in a heart-rending voice. Nobody answered. She compelled herself to take the coat down from the tree and put it round her shoulders. She immediately felt warmer and stopped shaking. I must find another one – for Sanka, she thought. And a rifle . . . that's the main thing, the rifle . . .

'I know a secret about you,' Sanka blurted out after her second gulp of vodka, and at once covered her mouth with her hand. She felt ashamed and rather sorry for the captain – and even more so for herself. She was alone and in near darkness with a man for the first time – not counting Viktor, and the father of one of the kindergarten children. The latter, arriving late one day to collect his child, whom his wife had already picked up, had grabbed hold of Sanka in the cloakroom and started touching her and taking all sorts of liberties. He had shameless, shining eyes, and, more important, his hands were strong and forceful. She could not fight him off, but he could do nothing with her anyway in the cloakroom, because there were still children and teachers left in the other groups, and the director herself had not yet gone home.

The next day at work she was afraid of meeting him, but his wife came for the child instead, and even when he reappeared he did not harass Sanka. At first this offended her, then it angered her, and she even started hanging around in the cloakroom for no reason, and once she even passed him, very close, and brushed him intentionally with her stomach, but he just laughed . . .

Viktor had turned out to be as inexperienced as she was, and although everything happened that night it didn't seem to mean much, and left no feeling of joy, but merely a vague awareness that she was no longer a snotty kid, but an adult. And now, looking at the captain and remembering what Maria Ivanovna had said about him, Sanka only half-believed her, and felt sure that something would happen – and she found it all rather worrying and frightening, but also very intriguing. And her whole body, unsettled by the motorcycle, was waiting and waiting, while the captain, dipping a baked potato in some salt, took a gulp of vodka from his tumbler, ate some *sauerkraut*, and seemed in no hurry whatsoever.

Maybe he really is an invalid? thought Sanka, and again recalled with horror the bombing raid, or rather, what she had seen during it: her own naked white body being laid into the wet and sticky earth; her breasts, shoulders and stomach being covered with the wormy soil – those same breasts and shoulders which she used to admire so much, standing naked before a mirror, to the envy and annoyance of Liya, who, on the contrary, seemed embarrassed by her own body.

Ain't I a beauty from head to foot
When I'm in my birthday suit . . .

Sanka had sung, pulling in her stomach and showing off her splendid hips in front of Liya.

And now it seemed fate itself had brought her here on the motorcycle, chosen from three hundred women . . .

'What other secrets do you know?' Gavrilov asked in a tired voice. 'Take your trousers off – they're all muddy. It's time to sleep.'

He looked at himself now from the side, as it were, and was disinclined and ashamed to start up any games or attempts at seduction. Neither his mood nor the time was right. He knew that even without them, under the blanket and coat, everything would work out.

The three hundred or so women, straggling along more than two kilometres of the road, had been tramping for over seven hours in the sharp icy snow, which suddenly turned to rain during the night. They were not really sure where they were going – whether to Moscow itself, or just closer to it, to other trenches – and carried their spades over their shoulders, with bags of meal or sugar suspended from them. Some had buckets, also full of provisions.

It was quiet. There were no trains rumbling, or aircraft screaming, or anybody shooting. The girls' commander walked with the last group, neither encouraging them nor reproaching them. She – and the others – were not so biddable that if she had been ordered to turn them back she would have done so, indeed they would have turned back themselves, without her command. And if they had been given rifles and ordered to lie down in the mud which now covered the ground, they would have lain down, and even those who could not shoot would have shot. Because their fatigue, and submissiveness, and anger had reached such a peak that this strength could last (and did last!) for years and years and even pass on to their children.

But nobody ordered them to turn round, and they were not given rifles, but trudged along the highway lugging their bags and buckets, until some thirty kilometres from the abandoned church they were stopped by some young fellows on motorcycles wearing the same kind of sheepskin coats as the dead lieutenant wore. They were told to leave their things in a wayside hut, and when dawn came – which was almost immediately – some were detailed to dig anti-tank ditches on either side of the road, while others had to dig up the ground and put it into sacks. And the women began shovelling the dirt as though that was precisely what they had come here for, and the previous day's bombardment, and the biting snow, and the thirty-kilometre walk through hail and rain had never existed, and as though all there was was earth, sticky at the top and brick-hard down below; and they regretted not having brought with them the picks and crowbars, from which, at the station, a hundred years ago, they had fled like devils from incense. It was just the same as yesterday and the evening before, except that the ground here was harder below the surface, the thin captain and the shy driver were not with them, and instead of the funny old man in the trenchcoat they were bossed around by a tall, sullen engineer.

17

'Are you still a virgin, or what?' asked Gavrilov in surprise. He had folded her in his arms – this open, joyful, submissive and impatient girl, who together with the vodka had beaten off his despair and tiredness, his fear for his family and country – and suddenly – hmm!

'No, don't worry,' she whispered eagerly, and pulled him towards her, pressing his shoulders. Inside, she felt pain, but only a slight pain, and so sweet, so alive and dear, that it immediately swept away all the yearning and torment that had been maturing in her for almost two years. It overcame her from within: she felt she would die, and was rapturously ready to die – but suddenly she was not dead, but was lying tired and happy on the bed with the captain beside her, and she was kissing his lips, still sour with cabbage.

'Oh, girls, I'm a woman now!' cried a joyful voice inside Sanka, and she felt like dashing out into the street, naked as she was, and shouting to the whole world: 'I'm a woman! I'm a woman!' And she couldn't care less if they said: 'But that's not your husband!' Let them! she thought. What good are husbands? Look how

Mother suffered with her drunkard. But I'm a woman! And I don't need a husband. What joy I feel inside of me. And husband or not, he's still mine – look, I can hug him if I feel like it, and squeeze him, and not let him go . . . Come on: look at me, stare at me, envy me!

Suddenly, quite out of the blue, she sang the words of a song: 'Captain, captain, give us a smile!' And Gavrilov did not recognize her voice, so changed was it, as though it had been kept hidden for a long time and had suddenly gushed out like spring water from a mountain; and for the first time in almost four months, since the outbreak of war, Captain Gavrilov burst out laughing, quietly and happily.

But about twelve kilometres away, as the crow flies, Liya, huddled in her greatcoat, was creeping along the edge of the wood in search of a spade and a rifle.

'Sanka!' she suddenly cried, but in such a wind she knew her voice would never reach the church. She had to search alone, and she did search, and search, forgetting the pain in her knee, which she had bruised on the machine-gun support. There weren't any rifles.

I'll have to take the machine-gun, Liya decided. I think it's meant for two – I saw one once at the civil-defence society. Perhaps I'll work it out. She went back to the second shell-crater and lifted the heavy Dyegtyaryov, with its nasty two-legged support, on to her shoulder. Swaying under the weight, she crossed the bridge, and, flagging, shouted: 'Sanka!'

She heard her voice resound along the bank – 'Aa-aankaa!' – but there was no other response. Liya set the machine-gun on the ground and flew up the hill to the church.

'Sanka! Sanka!' she shouted for all she was worth. 'Stop hiding, Sanka. Sanka, you devil!' she exclaimed, clenching her fists, and forgetting all other possible swear-words. Sanka did not reply. On the work-bench stood an oil-lamp which they had forgotten to extinguish, but the kerosene was finished and the wick was smoking, giving off little light.

Liya called Sanka's name again, but the vaulted ceiling merely mimicked her: 'Sa-a-anka!'

Where's our bag? she suddenly remembered. Seizing the lamp, she started fumbling around the church, but the bag was not there. All she found were some empty sugar and meal sacks lying about on the floor.

I'm going mad, thought Liya. No, I must have spent so long digging over there that she got impatient and left. I mean, I heard her calling to me. I'll go and look on the road.

But on the road there was no one either – only the wind and snow. Liya went back, but despite the snow and the desperate cold, she went into the church only for a moment, to pick up two empty sacks for cartridges, and then walked through the trenches looking for a spade. She found a spade and took it down to the bridge, lifted the machine-gun, and struggled across the river carrying the sacks, the spade and the machine-gun. Her eyes had now grown accustomed to the darkness. She found the dead soldier and started covering him up with earth. He no longer frightened her so much: after all, he had been alive only recently, and was probably a good, kind, courageous man; he had not deserted his wounded comrades. As she covered him up, she planned to find and bury the other four soldiers in the morning, when it got light, and then set out to the west with the machine-gun. She would be accepted even more readily with a machine-gun than with a rifle. And those rifles which she would find next morning, she would have to hide in the church. She might be lucky – no! not might, she definitely would be lucky – and she would find trucks or tanks heading for the front, which would take her *and* all the weapons. It was just a pity that Sanka had gone off with the bag containing her passport and Komsomol card. But it wasn't a catastrophe. They would believe her. She was a member of the Komsomol, after all. They could phone to Moscow – to the district committee, or the house-manager's office, or even the library. They would confirm it.

It was very cold, but Liya did not have the strength to go up to the church again, so she sat on the edge of a shell-hole and put her legs in a sack. 'I'll sit still for a while, and when it gets light I'll move.' Anxious about the machine-gun, which she did not understand but which she needed so badly, she covered it with the other sack, like a child.

I wonder how it works, though, she suddenly thought, and lifted the sack again.

At the top there was a circle. She knew that this was the magazine, which contained the cartridges, and evidently when the cartridges were used up the magazine had to be taken out and a new one put in. That was why you needed two soldiers – one to fire, the other to change the disc. But sometimes there was only one gunner left, and he still managed to keep firing somehow . . . This must be what you have to press – it's like on an ordinary rifle. But first you have to set up the stand. There is a poster about the Spanish Civil War: the man has been killed – he's lying on his back – and a black-haired girl has jumped down to operate the machine-gun. But that was a different type of gun – a Maxim, I think.

She kneeled down in the hole, pressed the two-legged support into the ground, placed her shoulder against the butt, and pulled the sere. Painfully and joyfully recoiling against her shoulder, the machine-gun spurted a flame into the wet night.

'Marvellous! Marvellous!' whispered Liya with a smile. She wrapped up the gun again. And began to wait for dawn.

The truck quickly reached the outskirts of Moscow, and only then – and in Moscow itself – did they have to stop at checkpoints. Soon they reached the hospital, and Ganya immediately jumped out and ran with her bag to the nearest tram stop.

'Where have you been? Down a mine?' asked the conductress, but Ganya ignored her. Her ears were still buzzing with explosions, machine-gun fire, and the groans of wounded women and soldiers. 'Antichrist': she remembered something terrible and incomprehensible that she had heard in her distant youth or childhood – something like today, she imagined, when it was rattling and wailing overhead, while inside you your stomach sank into your groin and your ribs into your navel, and struggled like a captured chicken.

She travelled as though in a dream, but managed to change trams at the right place, and then walked to the house, still in a dream, but chose the correct door and walked up to her boss's floor, unlocked the door of the communal flat, and then her boss's leatherette-upholstered door, sat down on the polished floor of the room, and finally opened her throat and poured out the whole of her miserable life in tears and screams.

'Oh!' she wailed, as though she herself had died and was weeping over her own body. She just kept repeating the same thing – 'Oh, oh,' – because her brain could understand no other words. Eventually, tired of crying, she fell asleep on the shining parquet floor and slept like a corpse in the empty flat until morning. In the morning she came to herself, filled a hot bath, and spent a long time scrubbing her now useless body. She scrubbed it and scrubbed it, vividly remembering what the women had said in the train. Then she opened the wardrobe, put on Karina's blouse and skirt (they were almost the same size), and sat down at the window to take up the hem on her mistress's old autumn coat. She had to be as quick as possible, so that she would have time to try and obtain ration cards, make a trip out to the house on the Iksha (there might be a letter from her nephews) and then visit Klanka's hospital to see if she was still alive. In short, there was a heck of a lot to do, and she had to keep her wits about her, and look clean.

'It's time to go,' said Gavrilov. Outside the dull grey window it was pouring with rain, but in the room it was just bright enough to see a little, and Gavrilov sat down to write a note to the telegraphist. 'Have a look and see if the stove's gone out,' he said over his shoulder to Sanka. 'We'll have to close up the pipe.'

She crawled out from under the blanket and greatcoat, big and white, crossed barefoot to the Dutch stove, and started poking the black embers.

He turned his head and looked in wonder at the well-built lass, not believing that it was she to whom he had spent the night unfolding his sorrows, his yearning for his wife and children, his bitterness at retreating, and in general all the misery of these four terrible months. She was so well-proportioned, as though drawn or modelled – not from clay, but from something living, soft and smooth.

She put her arms around him from behind, and he pressed the back of his head into her firm breasts, but he did not stop writing. 'Go and get dressed,' he said, 'or someone will see you naked.'

She loosened her hands, and from the pocket of his folded shirt which was on the table he took two red thirty-rouble notes and pinned them to his letter. Then he sighed and added a ten-rouble note to them.

'Quickly!' he said, and gave Sanka another hug, but carelessly this time, without the tenderness of the night, and she felt the joy stream out of her big young body like air from a burst volleyball.

Gavrilov felt her vexation in his back and affectionately stroked her cheek with his hand.

'You're all hot,' said Sanka, embracing him again.

I've caught a chill, thought Gavrilov, and said in a weary voice:

'Go and get dressed.' He was aching all over now. Thanks for the motorcycle, lieutenant, he thought for some reason.

'I'll be ready in no time!' exclaimed Sanka, dashing to the stove, where all her clothes were drying. Meanwhile he pushed the motorcycle out of the post office and warmed up the engine, and when Sanka came out he padlocked the door and put the key back under the railing. The street was awash with mud after the heavy rain, and at first the wheels just spun round, but eventually they left the God-forsaken village and rode out across the field in second gear, constantly getting stuck in ruts swollen with water.

'Oof-oof!' gasped Sanka, now embracing the captain as her own, and he in turn squeezed the motorcycle, which was responding badly to his weakened, feverish hands.

But about a mile before they reached the junction, where the track wound upwards for the last time, they saw the asphalt highway, along which a string of German tanks, from the distance like ducks, was moving towards Moscow. The first two tanks had already crossed the junction.

'That's it. They're through!' Gavrilov let out a sigh, and turned the motorcycle around.

'What if Liya didn't get away!' Sanka whimpered like a child. 'If she's taken prisoner . . . they'll kill her . . .'

'She got away, don't whine!' replied Gavrilov. He was feeling almost delirious, and only the danger helped to keep him alert.

But neither he nor Sanka knew that Liya, having dozed off only just before dawn, soaked and frozen stiff, had just been woken by the rumble of approaching German tanks, and, seeing the head and shoulders of a soldier standing up in the hatch of the leading tank, without second thoughts had opened fire. The bullets rebounded off the armour, and then the magazine jammed. While Liya was banging it with her fist, the soldier closed the hatch, and the tank rumbled off the roadway and with its right caterpillar track crushed the barrel of the machine-gun and Liya's red-haired head. It took no longer than a minute, but the other tanks meanwhile crossed the bridge, and the leading one was now the eighth in the line proceeding along the highway.

The wounded were driven to the first hospital inside the city boundary. Ganya disappeared at once, but Goshka, though frozen to the marrow, set about helping the hospital orderlies to carry stretchers, still with the loaded sub-machine-gun hanging from his neck. Then he and the driver were given hot cocoa to drink, and they set off for Gorky Street. There, in the Pass Office, the driver tried for a long time to get through to someone on the telephone, while Goshka sat nearby. But when the driver was finally allowed upstairs, some sergeant wearing the insignia of the internal military forces burst into the room and, without a word, took away Goshka's machine-gun.

Goshka sat weeping like a child for an hour, until the driver took him home in the frozen truck cabin. At home Goshka's aunt sighed over him all night, and in the morning dragged him off to the Kazan Station, where the evacuation was in full swing.

Almost until evening, Sanka and the captain exhausted themselves churning up the sodden fields, not daring to ride up on to the main road. When finally, furiously cursing the motorcycle, they did reach the road, they found it blocked with real anti-tank barriers and sacks packed with earth and clay.

Mastering his fever for a moment, Gavrilov was overjoyed, and recalled the Nazi propaganda leaflet again: 'Ha! So much for their "Russian ladies"! We'll see if it was such a waste of time!'

'What?' said Sanka, taken aback.

'Oh, it's just a song,' he said quietly, and she did not hear. A motorcyclist in a white, but now muddy, sheepskin coat checked their documents and allowed them past the barriers. A group of women, led by Maria Ivanovna, descended upon them from behind the barricade of sacks.

'So there you are?!'

Sanka jumped down from the pillion and hugged her commander as though they were sisters, or at least life-long friends, and Gavrilov drove on a little, but then braked and waited to see if she would run over to say goodbye. But Sanka, dejected and unhappy, was standing among the women and could not move, or perhaps was embarrassed to move.

'Where's the redhead?' asked Maria Ivanovna, but Sanka did not reply, and just as she was about to dash over to the captain, he gave up the wait. He suddenly remembered that he had never said goodbye to his wife and children; this disturbed him, and he opened the throttle as far as it would go. The bike reared like an unbroken horse, then tore off down the highway towards Moscow.

Gavrilov was tormented both by his fever and by the snub he felt at not being in command here. Work was steaming ahead without him: anti-tank barriers were being brought in, ditches dug, and great sackloads of earth piled up. And he, a tender-hearted army captain, had driven a hundred kilometres for the sake of some millet porridge, and look what happened.

Realizing that his chill could scarcely get any worse, he drove fast, and met a company of cadets marching to an old song about the 'blue waters of the Urals'. He stopped at the roadside and watched them pass by. They were marching in clean greatcoats, young and smooth-cheeked, but were very thin, as though underfed, and Gavrilov felt in his bones what would happen to them next day.

But the cadets were followed, and then overtaken, by a dozen or so trucks pulling ordnance and full of Red Army soldiers, and Gavrilov broke off his gloomy thoughts.

What's all this about? Pity? Pity? What does pity achieve? We've got *power*. And he thought again of the women, who were now digging the ground behind the anti-tank barriers. But then he wondered if it were not already too late: The peasant doesn't cross himself until the thunder comes, they say . . . His mind was skipping from one thought to another.

'And you, Gavrilov, are finished. You're burning as if you were in a steam-bath', he said aloud to himself, turning away from the wind blowing dust into his face. 'But Moscow is still safe. We'll smash Adolf before he gets there,' he said, and gave a shudder, because he had said exactly the same thing two days before, when the young driver was sitting beside him.

And as his fear for Moscow receded, so his heart ached even more for his family, for Simka and the children, whom he could do nothing to help.

'Just you be thankful if you come out of this fever alive,' he mumbled to himself, becoming less and less coherent. 'Now he'll be crossing himself . . . But he's not a peasant! And not even a Russian! Stop it, stop it!' he interrupted himself. 'Watch the road: it's slippery.'

At the city boundary he was asked for his documents again. He pulled them out, and with them the invoice for the millet and sugar he had obtained.

'Listen,' he said to the duty-officer returning his papers, 'What was the important announcement they were threatening to broadcast the day before yesterday?'

'Announcement?' The officer looked puzzled.

'You know . . . They were promising it in the morning, and then postponed it.'

'Ah!' the officer laughed. 'About the new opening hours for public baths and barbers' shops!' And he ran his hand over his young red cheeks, as though inviting the unshaven captain to do the same.

'They'll give me a wash and shave at the hospital,' said Gavrilov, and rode on. He could feel that his temperature was now over forty degrees.